"Gab

"Why not?" he demanded. "It's been between us from the moment you opened your door to me."

"No," Lisa pleaded.

He lowered his head. *"Yes,"* he whispered, taking full possession of her mouth. His raw, sensual hunger aroused her. He brushed his lips across her cheek, to her forehead, down the length of her throat. "So soft. So gentle. And these eyes...my little dove's eyes."

Her heartbeat faltered. Her breath locked in her throat. "Stop it," she gasped, twisting away from him. "Stop pretending...*lying*. No one but Jon ever said that about my eyes. And no one else knew he did!"

Gabriel remained completely, guiltily silent. And suddenly, Lisa guessed the unbelievable truth.

Dear Reader:

Happy summertime reading from everyone here! July is an extra-special month, because Nora Roberts—at long last—has written a much-anticipated Silhouette Desire. It's called *A Man for Amanda* and it's part of her terrific series, THE CALHOUN WOMEN. Look for the distinctive portrait of Amanda Calhoun on the cover.

And also look for the portrait of July's *Man of the Month,* Niall Rankin, on the cover of Kathleen Creighton's *In From the Cold*. Ms. Creighton has written a number of books for Silhouette Intimate Moments. Please *don't* miss this story; I know you'll love it!

There is something for everyone this month—sensuous, emotional romances written just for *you!* July is completed with other must-reads from the talented pens of your *very* favorites: Helen R. Myers, Barbara Boswell, Joan Johnston and Linda Turner. So enjoy, enjoy....

All the best,

Lucia Macro
Senior Editor

HELEN R. MYERS

WHEN GABRIEL CALLED

SILHOUETTE *Desire*®

Published by Silhouette Books New York

America's Publisher of Contemporary Romance

SILHOUETTE BOOKS
300 East 42nd St., New York, N.Y. 10017

WHEN GABRIEL CALLED

ISBN: 0-373-05650-8

First Silhouette Books printing July 1991

Printed in the U.S.A.

Books by Helen R. Myers

Silhouette Desire

Partners for Life #370
Smooth Operator #454
That Fontaine Woman! #471
The Pirate O'Keefe #506
Kiss Me Kate #570
After You #599
When Gabriel Called #650

Silhouette Romance

Donovan's Mermaid #557
Someone to Watch over Me #643
Confidentially Yours #677
Invitation to a Wedding #737
A Fine Arrangement #776

HELEN R. MYERS

lives on a sixty-five-acre ranch deep in the piney woods of East Texas with her husband, Robert, and a constantly expanding menagerie. She lists her interests as everything that doesn't have to do with a needle and thread. When she and Robert aren't working on the house they've built together, she likes to read, garden and, of course, outfish her husband.

For Marilyn Pappano and Laura Taylor,
two dear friends
who know what it's like to love special men

One

"**M**y name is Gabriel. Gabriel Ballesteros." The voice on the other end of the telephone line was as deep as it was hesitant after Lisa Howard's preoccupied greeting. "I was...a friend of Jon's."

Like a key being forced into a rusty lock, the words thrust deep into the scarred depths of her memory and met with resistance. Even as she dropped the red marking pencil she'd been using to correct her sixth grade's English papers, Lisa automatically tightened her other hand's grip on the phone's receiver. *No,* came the reply from an oppressed but still rational corner of her mind. Someone was playing a trick on her. It couldn't be. What she'd heard was wrong...imagined...impossible.

It had been three years since she'd been told she would never see Jon again. So much had happened since then, and she'd tried her best to forget—him, everything. But hearing this man's words now made her realize she had only been deceiving herself. She would never forget Jonathan Howard, no more than she would ever forgive him for deceiving her.

Three years. It felt like an eternity, and she'd been challenged by so much in that time, like relearning how to breathe, eat and sleep. How to take one day for what it was and let tomorrow take care of itself. How to care about life when the only man she had ever loved was no longer a part of it....

"Hello? Are you there?"

"Yes," Lisa replied, her thoughts jerked back to the present. Just as quickly, she realized she didn't know how to proceed. "I—I'm sorry. There's a series of storms passing through and the connection's bad." Indeed, no sooner did she say that than a flash of lightning made the house lights flicker, and several seconds later it was followed by an ominous roll of thunder. "Could you repeat that, please?"

"This *is* Mrs. Howard, is it not? Mrs. Jonathan Howard?"

The weary-sounding voice, with its hint of an accent—she guessed it was Hispanic—grew as cautious as her own. She didn't blame him. Obviously he was beginning to think he'd dialed the wrong number. "Yes, I'm Lisa Howard."

"My apologies for disturbing you at this late hour, Mrs. Howard. To repeat, my name is Gabriel Ballesteros. Jon and I were friends. Close friends."

Lisa hugged her waist with her free arm as protection against the shiver that raced through her. The laugh she attempted was more like a moan of pain. "I rather doubt that, Mr. Ballesteros. My husband wasn't the type of man to indulge in anything so socially *normal* as making friends."

"I knew him in South America, Mrs. Howard." Was that a hint of hurt she heard underlying his cultured voice? "He gave me a message for you."

Closing her eyes, Lisa slumped back in her chair. Dear heaven, if this was some kind of prank she didn't think she could survive it. She had been trying so hard to sever herself from the past. All right, maybe not as hard as she could have; but she'd purposely moved from Alexandria, Virginia, to Bentonville, Tennessee, to remove herself from the easy access of the civil, yet disturbing, people Jon had worked for. She was teaching again, making an attempt at achieving normalcy. Granted, her nights were still a torture and more often than not she felt as though she was functioning under some form of automatic pilot, yet each passing day saw her make a measure of progress.

Lisa sighed. She had no intention of losing that gained ground; but a message from Jon... "Why has it taken you so long to contact me?" she asked, reminding herself to be careful.

"There were...extenuating circumstances that made it impossible."

She had no doubt about that. If his line of work was anything like her husband's had been, then duty came first and everything else—friends, family, *love*—could wait. "All right, Mr. Ballesteros, what is it?"

"Not over the phone."

His quick curt censure gave Lisa a jolt and she straightened in her chair. Perhaps this was a legitimate call; he certainly sounded like the others, reserved, suspicious and, despite what she'd thought a moment ago, thoroughly lacking in any real human vulnerable qualities. Yes, he was probably one of them. Lifting her hand to her throat, she cautiously asked, "How then?"

"May I come to you?"

Lisa glanced toward the windows that lined one entire living-room wall. Darkness hid her chief concern with his request, namely that her cottage was deep in the woods of the Great Smoky Mountains. Right now all she could make out were the branches on the overgrown spruces, which were scraping against the windows as they yielded to each new gust of wind bringing yet another spring storm. She was also a good five miles from town and almost a mile from her nearest neighbor. Under those circumstances, she would be courting trouble to allow a stranger, even someone professing to be a friend, to come here.

"I don't think that's a good idea."

"In other words you're not alone."

Lisa saw her surprise and irritation in the window. He had nerve sounding censorious. "I beg your pardon? I don't believe it's any of your business whether I am or not."

"Forgive me. I meant no disrespect. In my excite— It was a selfish remark and I shouldn't have neglected to consider this might be an inconvenient time for you."

"Perhaps I can meet you in town tomorrow."

She heard a muffled hissing sound. Possibly a curse— or was he shivering? "Tomorrow is unacceptable. I must see you tonight. Please, Mrs. Howard. You have every right to be wary, but not of me. Jon would have never shared any information about the one person on earth he cared about with someone who would harm you."

As pain sliced through her heart, Lisa knew at least that much was true and, also, that she was beginning to believe him. More precisely, she *wanted* to believe him. Jon had always been vague and evasive when it came to discussing most aspects of his life. Even in their short time together, they had gone out several times before he'd told her anything about his work as a courier with the foreign service.

And it had been a lie.

Lisa raked her teeth over her lower lip. "Mr. Ballesteros, I'm sorry if I sound as though I'm putting you off. It's just that I don't live on a well-traveled road and in this weather—"

"I'm deeply touched by your concern, but I assure you I'll have no problems managing the drive."

This time he sounded as if he might be smiling. Small wonder, she told herself, since her lame excuse sounded ridiculously transparent even to her own ears. Why not get it over with? The man was clearly determined. And it wasn't as though she would get any rest with something unresolved like this churning around in her mind.

"All right. Tonight then. Let me give you directions."

"That won't be necessary. I know how to find you."

For seconds after the line went dead, Lisa continued to sit there. It was only the eventual click and subsequent return of the dial tone that brought her back to reality.

She replaced the receiver in its cradle at the corner of her desk. And that's that, she thought uneasily. Ready or not he was coming. *Oh, Jon...*

She focused on her left hand. Its fine tremor accented the play of light on her wedding ring and she recalled the day he'd purchased it for her. He had tried to talk her into choosing something more extravagant, but she'd argued it would have been like asking a country girl—which was basically what she considered herself—to walk around wearing a tiara. Besides, the moment she'd spotted this one no other would do. The braided design seemed symbolic of how, from the moment they'd met, their lives were uniquely completely entwined.

That's why she still wore it. Nothing had changed.

Somehow, even after three years of living without him, despite her bitterness about learning how naive and gullible she'd been, she still felt the connection. In his periodic phone calls, Jon's former associate and friend, Mason Sennett—the one man she felt she could trust among all those government sharks—kindly hinted it was time to let go, to get on with her life. Her friends were less subtle but equally concerned. Though she appreciated everyone's good intentions, she also found them frustrating.

Why couldn't they understand? What she'd felt for Jon had been so difficult to describe; it seemed to surpass even the most encompassing boundaries of love. It wasn't as though she had been a child. Back when they'd met, as today, she was generally known as a serious sensible woman. A dedicated teacher. Meeting him and falling under the power of those hypnotic dark brown eyes, his fever-inducing touch, had been suddenly stunning. Now she could admit to even feeling a bit frightened.

He'd introduced her to an insular world where passion ruled and her senses were systematically seduced by his wit and charm, his attentiveness and his uncompromising sexuality. He'd breached her laughingly vulnerable defenses and turned her into a love-struck sensual creature she'd hardly recognized.

Just months after turning twenty-five, only weeks after meeting him, they'd been married. Before her twenty-sixth birthday she'd been told she was a widow.

How could she "get on" with her life, consider another relationship, when this one had been everything she could ever have dreamed of?

But, she reminded herself, it had been more dream than reality.

A familiar ache gripped her heart, and she took a deep breath in an attempt to ease the pain that never went away completely. It had been Mason Sennett who'd eventually relented and shared with her what truths he could. He'd acknowledged Jon had been affiliated with a covert government agency and had been their chief troubleshooter; the one who went into a delicate and usually dangerous environment and did what had to be done.

For the first time, she'd learned his assignment had taken him to Argentina; but what the job had been, Mason wouldn't say, and how Jon died, he couldn't explain. Something had gone wrong and he'd disappeared, vanished off the face of the earth.

Despite Mason's warning that she not hold out false hope, Lisa had ignored her shock, put aside her hurt pride and remained steadfast in her faith that good news would prevail. Jon would return. It seemed all that was important.

Then, a few weeks later, a body was found. Due to its condition, no conclusive identification could be made, but Mason admitted everything pointed to the obvious. It was Jon.

Lisa's gaze was involuntarily drawn to the porcelain-framed photograph beside the phone. Their wedding photograph; one of the few times Jon hadn't managed to avoid getting his picture taken. And why hadn't she picked up on that quirk? she brooded for the umpteenth time. Why hadn't she found it odd that he kept slipping her camera out of her hands, while they'd been on their Caribbean honeymoon, insisting instead that *she* pose before the various blooming shrubberies and scenic spots? No, she'd been gullible, instead preferring to believe he thought her beautiful and that it gave him pleasure to see her happily accepting a purchase from a vendor and cavorting with the children.

"Why couldn't you at least have shared a little of the truth with me?" she whispered, tracing her index finger across the sweep of black hair she'd loved to stroke. She always thought he dominated this picture, even though he was looking at her and not the camera. His bold dark features were a stark contrast to her fairness. How proud she'd been when they would walk into the hotel's dining room and women stole envious glances their way.

She'd been so caught up with him, she would gladly have lived with his work, the necessity of secrets, whatever it took. But he hadn't given her the option to choose.

And now a man named Gabriel Ballesteros had a message for her. Words that Jon had spoken. If she was smart, she would have told Mr. Ballesteros that she wasn't interested, that she'd already dedicated three years of her life to mourning a man who in reality had been more a stranger than husband, and she was tired, tired, *tired*. But, heaven help her, she hadn't been able to do it.

She glanced again at her reflection in the window. "Well, you'll scare him away before he can tell you anything," she muttered to the tawny-haired wide-eyed woman staring back at her.

Tawny—that was Jon's word; dirty-blond seemed a more accurate description, and considering that she hadn't run a brush through her hair since this morning, it looked more limp than reed straight, which had been another of his pet annotations. It also didn't help that the lipstick she'd replaced after lunch had long since been nibbled off; the resulting lack of color only emphasized the shadowy smudges under her eyes—a permanent feature these days.

Pushing herself away from the desk and the remaining English papers that still needed to be marked, she rose, intending to freshen up. But before she could take a step, her dog, Pilot, lifted himself from his resting place at her feet and blocked her way. He was black, part German shepherd and part anyone's guess. Black Angus, she often suggested to him when his healthy appetite sent her to the market before her normal shopping day.

"You sense something's up, don't you?" she murmured, cupping a hand beneath his jaw to consider his curious adoring eyes. As always, looking at him brought a wistful smile to her lips. The moment she'd seen those amber eyes, gazing at her from the other side of the dog pound's wire fence, she knew she had to take him home. At the time they'd reminded her of her own, for they, too, had reflected loneliness and fear. At least she'd been able to improve his lot in life.

"We're about to have company, my friend, so I expect you to be on your best behavior," she told him, though she knew she was wasting her time, since her voice lacked any serious trace of authority. "You can start by getting out of my way, so I can go make myself presentable."

In the end she was forced to sidestep him on her way to the bathroom, where she splashed cold revitalizing water on her face. Then she briskly dragged a brush through the heavy fall of her hair.

As a child, she'd yearned for curls, but not after she'd met Jon, who said he fell in love with her waist-length hair first. The Saturday they'd met, he'd spotted her leaning over a used-book rack at the Alexandria street fair they'd both attended.

Accepting the stab of pain that memory brought, Lisa added a touch of rose-colored lipstick to her lips before considering the results. Would Jon be attracted to her now? She seemed a ghost of her former self. It went beyond the lack of makeup and pale skin; always slender, she now bordered model thin, and her skirt and blouse—attractive though the powder blue was—hung on her uninspiringly. Sometimes when the wind was particularly strong, it tugged at her hair—now only reaching the middle of her back—and tested her balance. It was at times like that when even *she* had to admit to some modicum of concern. But no matter how she tried, her appetite failed to improve.

She gazed into the serious gray eyes reflected in the mirror, knowing what would change all that. Maybe there was another reason for Mr. Ballesteros's visit; that would explain his reluctance to talk over the phone. He could be bringing her more than a message from Jon; he could be bringing news that Mason Sennett's sources had been wrong and that Jon was alive!

"Stop it," she whispered, pressing her palms to her eyes.

Jon was *dead* and that was the end of it.

Regaining her control and smoothing her eyebrows with her fingers, she headed back to the living room, Pilot following her like a shadow. Reminding herself that though she might not be much for primping, she at least liked to keep a neat house, she hurriedly swept her briefcase off the coffee table and the sofa pillows off the floor and back onto the couch. The week's worth of newspapers scattered about had to settle for being piled on top of the already full basket of magazines beside the easy chair.

As she worked, she thought about the man who was coming to see her. She wished she'd pressed him for more information about himself. What were those "extenuating circumstances" that had kept him from contacting her sooner? Who was he really? And where exactly had he been calling from?

She wondered if she should ask him for some identification before letting him into the house. On second thought the idea struck her as ludicrous, since even she had heard how easily such things could be falsified. And considering how reluctant he'd been to give information over the phone, it was clear he had at least some passing knowledge of Jon's type of work. The reminder of that sent a shiver racing down her spine. Surely he didn't suspect her phone was tapped? What boring surveillance that would be for some poor soul. Often the thing went days without being used. No, she was definitely letting her imagination get carried away. He was probably just trying to be solicitous of her feelings.

Finished with straightening the room, she headed for the kitchen to put on a pot of coffee. Though it was May and the Great Smoky Mountains were warming rapidly, the nights remained crisp. If her visitor had managed to get wet in these intermittent downpours, as that shiver or whatever it was had suggested, he would welcome something hot to ward off the chill.

A sudden flash of lightning once again sent the lights flickering on and off, and she stiffened awaiting the inevitable crack of thunder. When it came, it rattled the entire cottage. Sitting with his body pressed to her leg, Pilot growled.

"I know, boy. It's getting to me, too, but the worst of it will pass soon enough."

Lisa finished filling the pot. Then she set it on the stove and adjusted a medium flame beneath it. But before she could bend over to give her pet a reassuring pat, he bounded to his feet and began barking.

Lisa's heart gave a startled lurch. It was barely ten minutes since the call. In good weather it took her at least fifteen to maneuver the steep winding road to her school, which was in the center of town. It couldn't be him. He would have to have phoned her from Mack's Garage at the base of the mountain.

Yet off went Pilot, running to the front door, his fur standing on end as it always did when he was particularly agitated. After running her hands down over her straight skirt and then pressing one to her thudding heart, Lisa followed and turned on the outside light.

She could hear the rain intensifying as she fiddled with the chain and the dead bolt. If she didn't hurry, the poor man was going to drown, she thought, finally succeeding and jerking open the door. In the last second, she remembered to grab Pilot's leather collar.

A wall of water running over the leaf-clogged gutters hampered her view of the figure walking toward her. *Walking.* He had to be crazy, she thought, squinting in an attempt to see him more clearly. Adding to the noise level, Pilot broke into a tirade of barking and lunged against her hold.

"Down, Pilot," she commanded, before calling to the man. "Hurry!"

His pace didn't change and belatedly she realized why. He was clearly favoring his left leg; however, even that wasn't what sent Lisa's heart into her throat. It was his build, his darkness—something about his silhouette that was undeniably, strikingly familiar.

As he stepped through the waterfall bisecting her front stoop, Lisa clapped a hand to her mouth to stifle a cry. Then lightning stuck somewhere close and just as the earth began to vibrate with ear-splitting thunder, everything went black.

Two

The sound of Lisa's muffled cry was obliterated by the storm; but her shock must have transmitted itself to Pilot, who broke free of her hold and leapt against the man in the doorway. In the ensuing struggle, arms tangled with arms and paws, while both humans tried to avoid sharp canine teeth. Throughout, Pilot's snarls and barks, along with the sounds from the raging storm, kept the noise level deafening.

"Damnation. *Down, Pilot!*"

Both Lisa and her pet went still at their visitor's sharp authoritative command. An instant later the lights came back on.

Man, woman and dog, caught in a three-way stare, remained motionless for several more seconds. Then, with a growl followed by a whimper, Pilot sat down at the feet of the man who'd rebuked him.

It was too much—Pilot's sudden docility, the violent weather, this shocking first view of the stranger. Suddenly, everything in Lisa's scope of vision began to spin crazily. As she felt her knees buckle, the stranger grabbed her by her upper arms and pushed her back against the door.

"Take a deep breath," he demanded gruffly. "Do it. I would hate for you to discover the unfortunate truth that I'm currently in no condition to play the gallant. Good. Now another."

Though Lisa did as he directed, she never took her eyes off him; she barely even blinked. She was afraid that if she did they might start playing tricks on her again. But now, as he stood under the entryway light, she could see how wrong, how utterly impossible it was to have thought, even for a few heart-stopping moments, that he was Jon. She wasn't, however, completely calmed. Closer inspection only brought a different kind of emotional trauma.

The poor man had obviously been through some kind of hell of his own. Someone admirably skilled in medical science had done his best to help him, but the left side of his face bore evidence of reconstructive surgery and skin grafting. And, of course, there was the black patch over his left eye that only emphasized how terrible his injury must have been. Dear Lord, Lisa thought, her heart wrenching in grief that anyone should suffer like this, what horror had he experienced?

Her expression must have mirrored her thoughts. After muttering a barely audible oath, he said, "I should have warned you over the phone what to expect."

Bitterness gave his already gruff voice a hard edge and made her ashamed of her all-too-human reaction of staring. When he tried to turn away, an involuntary sound of protest broke from her throat. "No! Please," she entreated, impulsively reaching out to him. Her fingers grazed his whisker-roughened jaw. His response—a sudden stiffening and wariness, like an injured animal who'd grown suspicious of all human contact—spawned the strangest urge in her to weep. "Please don't turn away. It's the weather and the lights. This is the worst storm I've experienced since I've been here, and I'm afraid it has me more tense than usual."

When their gazes locked again, Lisa felt as though every nerve ending in her body took notice. Familiar— it was the only word that came to mind to describe the warm pulling sensation that followed. She felt as though she should be embracing this man like an old friend. But that was impossible. She'd never met him before in her life.

It was the way he was looking at her, she swiftly assured herself. With that thickly-lashed brown eye, so dark and intense, it was inevitable that her thoughts would turn fanciful. She'd been reminded of Jon and the way he used to look at her, that's all. But rather than feel embarrassed, Lisa was overcome by a deep-seated sadness.

As if he could read her mind, Gabriel Ballesteros dropped his gaze to his hands that—despite a subtle shaking—still firmly held her. Swallowing, he released his hold. Yet apparently, even that wasn't enough. He took a step backward.

"How did you know my dog's name?" she asked, thinking that for all she knew he could have been stalking her for days. No, she admitted, her question was really only to cover the silence that suddenly, like the rain, seemed to possess its own heartbeat.

"You said it when I was coming up the walk."

"Oh." To hide her chagrin, she glanced down at her pet and saw him squirm closer to their visitor, sniff his shoes, his pants. As he explored, Pilot's wagging tail maintained a steady drumbeat connecting again and again with the wall. Lisa twisted her lips into an ironic smile. "Congratulations. Ordinarily he doesn't care for strangers."

"Ordinarily I'm shy of animals with teeth larger than my own."

Shy? Now there was a word Jon would never have used—at least not in reference to himself. Again Lisa lifted her gaze, only to find herself once more in danger of succumbing to the man's hypnotic scrutiny.

Blinking hard to break the spell, she groped behind her for the doorknob. "Where are my manners? Come in before you catch pneumonia."

"I'm already creating a mess as it is," he replied, glancing down to consider the wood floor, where a puddle was indeed spreading.

"It doesn't matter. Let me get you a towel so you can dry your face and hair." As she nodded reassuringly, he stepped further into the entryway and she shut the door behind him.

Denying him the opportunity to protest any more—and he looked like he was ready to—she hurried around the corner and to the bathroom. When she returned, she was carrying a huge green bath sheet, the kind she still bought because Jon had preferred them.

Her guest hadn't moved from where she'd left him. Beyond the indecisiveness of his stance, he appeared completely exhausted. Briskly unfolding the lush towel, she offered it to him, then beckoned toward the living room.

"Come sit down."

"I don't want to be a—"

"Bother. Yes, you've already made that clear. But a little water isn't going to hurt anything. Besides, you don't look as though you'll be able to last on your feet much longer."

She watched as he seemed to deliberate over his options and finally accepted the wisdom of what she'd said. Following her, he slumped gratefully into the nearest seat, the navy blue easy chair, and closed his eye. Lisa used the opportunity to study him. No, she had been wrong to think there was a strong resemblance between him and Jon. Despite the similarities— and there were several—the difference was undeniable. She'd been fooled by their mutual darkness, the exotic coloring that suggested any number of cultures, from Latin to Greek to Middle Eastern. But Jon had worn his hair relatively short because he'd found its natural wave annoying. There also hadn't been a hint of gray in it. Gabriel Ballesteros's hair, though now drenched and plastered to his head, curled around the collar of his windbreaker and the white shirt he wore beneath it; and numerous slashes of gray dramatically framed his face, which made it all the more difficult to judge his age. This man looked as if he'd already celebrated his fortieth birthday. Perhaps one or two more.

His physical condition added to his older appearance. Like Jon he was of medium height, but he looked gaunt, almost emaciated, as if he'd been ill. Or, she thought with some unease, imprisoned. Considering the reports that kept appearing in the newspapers the latter speculation wasn't very farfetched. So much of the Southern Hemisphere seemed to be in turmoil these days, which only added to the difficult conditions—

both economic and political—for those who lived there. A jail term or illness was feasible. Whichever, it had cost him dearly.

Yet what drama his face held. Jon's face had been lean, too; however, that's where most of their similarities ended. Gabriel Ballesteros's features were more stark and angular than her late husband's. Almost hawklike. Jon's nose had been straight with no imperfections in the bridge. Lisa suspected that the bump marring her guest's was a result of a blow rather than heredity. But not because he gave the impression of being someone who got into fights; on the contrary, he seemed to be the type of man who preferred to use his head rather than his fists. Still, after having spent all those weeks and months dealing with men whose job it was to deal with the darker, rarely commendable sides of humanity, she'd come to recognize a certain quality they all shared. Restrained lethality. Gabriel Ballesteros had that look.

He also had a high brow and deep-set eyes, and his pronounced cheekbones were even more dramatic because of his gaunt condition. His mouth, however, had her once again staring. Jon's, too, had been thin lipped, yet sensual. And he'd also had the habit of compressing them into a hard line when he was tense or concentrating.

And so do a thousand other men, you fool. Stop looking for similarities as if you're hoping to find them. Didn't you once say that if he had returned, you would have left him?

Fingering her wedding band like a string of worry beads, Lisa raised her gaze to find herself once more meeting Gabriel Ballesteros's searching look.

"There are those who said your Jon and I favored each other," he murmured in that gruff scratchy rumble that did nothing to detract from his cultured accent.

"You do share a similar coloring."

"Ah. A diplomat." His gaze grew more probing. "Do I repulse you?"

Lisa's self-castigation turned to dismay. "No! How could you think that?"

In slow motion he inched the towel along his jaw and down his throat, clearly relishing its feel. "After spending considerable time away from the mainstream of civilization, I've recently had ample opportunity to gauge people's receptiveness to this," he said, gesturing to the left side of his face. "Children seem particularly disturbed by it. At an airport one went running to her mother screaming she'd seen a monster."

"Children can be cruel," Lisa replied without hesitation, inwardly annoyed that the child's parent hadn't corrected the youngster right away and apologized. "And they're not always good at looking beyond the outer shell of things." Realizing how critical that must sound, Lisa grimaced. "I'm a schoolteacher and, while I love my work, experience has forced me to broaden my once idealistic opinion of young people in general."

"What, then, would you say would be an *accurate* description of my persona?"

"Wounded but—"

"But—?"

"Noble." The look that earned her caused a long dormant excitement to stir within her. Unsettled, even embarrassed by the feeling, Lisa retreated by sidestepping him and edging toward the kitchen. "You looked chilled to the bone. I was making coffee when you arrived. If you'll excuse me, I'll go see if it's ready.''

Without waiting for a reply, she escaped to tend to that chore. Of all the inane things to say, she berated herself as she turned off the flame beneath the percolating pot. The man was going to think she was an addle-brained romantic. It hadn't been necessary to run out of there like a scared rabbit, either. She might not be the beauty Jon had called her, but she received her share of male attention. And just because she wasn't interested in encouraging it didn't mean she had to behave as though she was fresh from a convent. Besides, he hardly appeared in any condition to pounce.

Reminded of the way he'd been shivering, she eyed the cups and saucers she'd just retrieved from the cupboard. He would probably be grateful to have something more substantial to hold on to. Exchanging the fragile china for sturdy oversize mugs, she poured the aromatic coffee into both, only to find herself hesitating over adding cream and sugar. She preferred hers black and unsweetened; however, he looked like he could use nourishment from whatever source was available. Placing cream and sugar containers, as well as their mugs, on a tray, she carried everything to the living room.

Pilot had settled on the braided rug in the middle of the floor and was resting his muzzle on his front paws. He continued to watch their guest as if he wanted to put him under a microscope. He wasn't the only one, Lisa thought dryly. She herself had a million and one questions she wanted to ask Gabriel Ballesteros.

In her absence, he'd removed his windbreaker and she spotted it hanging on the coat-closet doorknob. Pilot didn't seem to mind that the stranger had been moving around. Was she going to have to start worrying about his prowess as a watchdog? she wondered, setting the tray on the coffee table.

"*Dios,* so soft," Gabriel Ballesteros murmured, reluctantly lifting his head from the depths of the towel and draping it around his neck. "I don't know when I last felt anything this luxurious."

"They don't have fabric softener where you came from?" she asked, attempting to relax them both with gentle humor.

"They barely have towels," he replied drolly.

"It sounds as though you lived in a very remote place." Or a poor one. "Cream and sugar?"

"A little of both. *Gracias,*" he added, after she'd stirred in those ingredients and handed him the mug.

"Drink it slowly—it will still be very hot," Lisa said, noting he'd deftly ignored her first statement. Wondering why, she picked up her own mug and sat in the high-backed chair on his left.

He took a tentative sip and exhaled with satisfaction. "But excellent."

"Not too sweet?"

"What a question to ask a man who's lived without any form of sweetness for longer than he cares to remember. I'll take what I can get."

The words, as well as a certain intimate nuance in his voice, caused Lisa to drop her gaze to her own coffee. This wouldn't do, she told herself. She was happy to do what she could to make him comfortable, but it wouldn't be wise if she gave him the wrong impression.

She blew softly across the surface of her own coffee before taking a tentative sip. "I have many questions, Mr. Ballesteros," she said at last.

"I don't doubt it."

"I should begin by saying that your caution on the phone disturbed me."

"*Perdón, señora.* It was unintentional. Old habits linger whether one intends them to or not."

"Then I am correct in assuming you and my husband were in the same line of work?" she asked, cautiously.

That earned her a startled look from her guest. "Jon . . . told you about his work?"

Lisa's smile was bitter. "He told me nothing, Señor Ballesteros," she replied, vaguely wondering how much of her college Spanish she still remembered. In her junior year she'd switched to French, dreaming of one day touring her favorite foreign land. Jon had been the one fluent in Spanish. "What he did was lie," she continued, momentarily allowing her hurt to overcome her sadness. "But that, of course, was a belated discovery."

She stroked her thumb over the rim of the mug to wipe away a smudge of lipstick. It would probably make absolutely no sense to him, but she was as hesitant to share what little she knew of Jon as she was desperate to learn whatever more she could. "Oh, you might as well know it all. You see, we met and fell in love impossibly fast. He told me he was a courier with the foreign service and that his job required extensive traveling. It sounded reasonable and—for a girl who'd been born and grew up in rural West Virginia—wonderfully romantic. Of course, at the time I was thinking more with my heart than my head."

"Which is as it should be when one is falling in love."

His voice was a rough caress, like brushed suede over the scar tissue surrounding her heart, tempting her to tell him more. Lisa tried to assure herself that anyone listening to that intriguing accent would have been affected, but even so she felt oddly guilty.

Good Lord, why? she asked herself in the next instant. It wasn't as if it was possible to be unfaithful to a ghost.

"Yes, that's what I've tried to convince myself of, too," she admitted self-consciously. "But it was no excuse not to ask more questions. I realize he was probably only trying to protect me—at least I have to believe that was the case."

"You shouldn't doubt it. In my opinion he was wise."

"He was wrong!" At his look of surprise, Lisa took a deep breath to temper the agitation in her voice. "Excuse me. I shouldn't be troubling you with my problems. You obviously have more than your share to deal with as it is."

"That doesn't exempt me from feeling... compassion for what you must have experienced." He lowered his gaze to his mug. "Tell me—how did you ultimately learn of your husband's true occupation?"

"Persistence. And the kindness of a man who'd been his friend. A man who had a family of his own, so he could empathize with what I was going through." Lisa smiled wistfully as she thought of the Sennett's little boy and infant girl she had ached to hug and coddle when Mason insisted on bringing her home to dinner just before she moved from Alexandria. "His name is Mason Sennett. He was Jon's inside contact with the agency for whom they both worked."

"Inside contact..."

"Mmm. Sounds awfully vague, doesn't it? He never did expand on that much, but I assume it was a nice way of saying he was Jon's boss."

"I see." Gabriel took another careful sip of his coffee. "So it was Sennett who suggested that Jon was much more than a simple courier."

"He didn't suggest, he told me. He explained how Jon was the agency's troubleshooter—there's a euphemism for you—and that he routinely handled the agency's more complex assignments."

"Your bitterness is, perhaps, not without merit, *señora,* but I can't help wondering whether you would have been able to deal with that knowledge had you known it sooner," Gabriel said, his tone flat.

"Of course I would. I think. All right, I don't know," she admitted, when he continued to consider her with that unblinking and indiscernible look.

"No," he agreed after a long pause. "And apparently Jon was unwilling to take the risk of losing you."

"Mr.—Señor Ballesteros, if you don't mind—"

"Gabriel, please."

Deciding she couldn't swallow another drop of coffee no matter how hard she tried, Lisa placed her mug on the table. "Gabriel. Perhaps it would be best to focus on the reason you contacted me. On the phone, you told me you have a message from my husband. Will you tell me it now?"

"As you like."

"Were they..." It was incredibly difficult, but she had to know. "Were they his last words?"

"Would it matter so much if they were?"

Lisa moistened her lips and fingered the brass buttons on the armrest of her chair. "I understand your skepticism and I wish I could explain my feelings to you, but I can't even understand them myself. However, yes, I would like to know."

"They were his last words."

Somewhere deep inside her, Lisa felt her last flicker of hope snuffed out. "Somehow I knew you would say that. Then you *were* there when it happened." Though it wasn't exactly a question, Gabriel inclined his head. "And there was no chance that an error was made and that it wasn't really he who—"

"His assailants made sure there would be no walking away from the car bomb when it went off," Gabriel said bluntly before she could finish voicing her oft-dreamed wish.

Lisa could feel the blood drain from her face. "A...bomb?"

Gabriel muttered an expletive in Spanish and put down his mug. He began to reach out to her, but seeing her suddenly freeze, he quickly withdrew. Gripping both ends of the towel, he slumped back in the chair. "I thought you knew," he said, his voice a strange mixture of apology and anger. "I thought they...someone would have told you."

Shock and grief created a band around Lisa's throat making the simple act of breathing difficult. "At first they only told me he was missing, but that they had strong reason to believe he'd been killed. It was a few weeks before they found a body. I don't remember why it took so long—my mind was in a daze by then. It might have been the terrain or something. At any rate," she said, her voice growing more and more unsteady, "he was so badly injured, they couldn't make a positive identification. For some reason I thought that could mean... I'm not sure what I thought it meant."

She couldn't stay seated. Jumping out of the chair like a windup toy, she walked aimlessly, eventually finding herself staring out one of the windows, past the rivulets of water coursing down the panes of glass, into the darkness.

A bomb. Dear heaven. Of all things she'd imagined, it hadn't been that. She closed her eyes, praying that death had come quickly. She'd seen television news footage of incidents where bombs had been used. Rarely did anyone survive them and never, it seemed, without serious injury. That miracle was restricted to movies.

"Are you all right?"

Startled to hear him directly behind her, Lisa spun around. She hadn't heard him move. In her low-heeled pumps, she was almost at eye level with his enigmatic gaze; only the whiteness of his knuckles as he gripped the towel told her that he wasn't as in control as he would have liked her to think.

"You actually saw it happen, didn't you?" she whispered, searching his face.

"Why do you insist on putting yourself through even more grief?"

"Because he was my husband."

"He wouldn't have wanted you to dwell on his passing. You're vibrant, young—"

"Please don't tell me what I am, Señor Ballesteros. I need to have some answers. If you won't help me, I'll go back to the United States government with this new information and demand answers from them."

As she began to turn away from him, Gabriel took hold of her arm. "All right, *yes*. I was there."

Once again Lisa faced him fully. "Tell me everything."

Gabriel shook his head, his expression a warring mixture of frustration and admiration. "Jon never told me his bride was such a headstrong woman."

"It's a recent development," she replied, lifting her chin in a show of determination. "I learned it the hard way, after discovering that pulling on my forelock or acting demure wasn't going to get me the answers I wanted."

Aware that he was trying to intimidate her, she tried to outstare him. Just when she thought she was going to have to give up and lower her eyes, he muttered something under his breath and turned away from her.

"We were leaving the place where we'd been staying," he began, the words bursting forth like an eruption of bullets from a machine gun. "We'd gotten information that his cover was—how do you say it?—blown. He was no longer safe in Argentina. I was going to drive him to the airport, dispose of the car and go underground myself. He was going to start the car while I went down to the road to make sure the way was clear. On my way back to join him, it happened."

Though she'd had years to prepare herself, Lisa had to press her fingers to her lips to stifle a sob. "Tell me, please tell me, that it was over quickly."

"I do not believe he suffered."

It wasn't much, but Lisa tried to take comfort in that. She reached for the tiny solid gold heart she still wore around her neck. It had been the last gift Jon had given her. But as she clutched the smooth pendant between her fingers, she experienced a rush of guilt and shame.

Here she was feeling sorry for herself and she hadn't offered an ounce of sympathy or gratitude toward the man who'd been her husband's friend. Reaching out, she touched his shoulder. "That's how you sustained your injuries, wasn't it?"

Slowly, reluctantly, he turned to face her. "It was shrapnel that cost me my eye and injured my leg. The burns came from trying to reach the car and get him out.''

Lisa's eyes burned with fresh tears. She shook her head. No words would be enough to make up for what he must have suffered. "You said he went quickly, but you . . . the pain . . ."

"A second blast knocked me unconscious."

"Oh, dear Lord. I'm sorry," she whispered, aching for him. "I'm so sorry."

Helpless not to, her gaze was drawn to the left side of his face. Their closeness allowed her to see the pinkish areas where grafting had been necessary, and the faint scarring at his hairline and along his jaw marked the path of the surgeon's stitches. He would never regain the face he'd had before—that much was evident—but he was wrong to believe his appearance was repulsive, as he'd suggested.

She parted her lips to tell him so, only to realize that he was staring at her mouth. Her heart made a strange fluttering movement. The room expanded and compressed around them. Lisa knew it was time to move away and change the subject, but for the life of her, she couldn't make her legs budge; they seemed glued to the hardwood floor.

He wanted to kiss her. She didn't need a microscope to see the reality of that in his eyes, but what surprised her more was that she *wanted* him to. It was insane, of course; he was a virtual stranger—the man who'd tried to save Jon's life, yes, but still she'd always been reserved around people she didn't know well. Not since Jon had she been tempted to abandon her conservative behavior, and she'd vowed never to allow herself such a reckless kind of passion again.

It was that promise to herself that allowed her to withdraw a step and avert her gaze. "Your, um, coffee will get cold," she murmured, her voice sounding as if she'd swallowed a spoonful of thick honey.

Gabriel slowly withdrew, also. Reluctantly, Lisa thought. The way he lowered himself into his chair made him look like a man bearing the weight of the world on his shoulders. She was tempted to ask him if he didn't have a suitcase in his car with a change of clothes, so he could at least get out of that soaked white shirt and black slacks. But considering their condition, she had a feeling he'd been wearing them for more than a day and probably had little else to replace them. He would undoubtedly be embarrassed to have to admit as much to her.

"I should tell you Jon's message now," he said, after downing most of his coffee.

He said it as if he was reminding himself why he was there. Lisa felt a strong urge to reassure him; after all, the kiss hadn't happened. Then again it was sometimes better to leave well enough alone.

She pressed a hand to her unsteady stomach and nodded. "When, um, when did he give it to you?"

"Just before we headed outside. Perhaps he had a premonition. Who can say?" Setting down his mug, he leaned forward in the chair and clasped his unsteady hands tightly between his knees. "He asked, should things go badly, that I try to contact you. He wanted me to let you know there wasn't a day that passed when you weren't in the forefront of his mind. He also said to tell you he loved you—with all his heart and soul. And he hoped that someday you would learn to forgive him for having kept so much of himself from you."

Lisa turned away and tightly shut her eyes. She wanted to cry; her entire body ached to purge the grief inside her. But suddenly the tears that had been a constant threat wouldn't come.

So it was finally, truly over. Of course, she'd always known in the back of her mind that Jon was gone, but Gabriel had just given her what she needed to let go and lay the past to rest. Jon *had* loved her; it didn't excuse the deceit, but it made her feel less cheated, less of a fool. She could go on with the job of living. She would survive.

A low groaning sound made her spin around. Gabriel's shaking was growing more severe and he was trying to push himself to his feet.

Lisa rushed to help. "What's wrong?" she demanded, steadying him.

"It's nothing. I'll be fine once I find a...once I leave."

"Don't be ridiculous. You can't drive in this condition." She touched his forehead and discovered he was burning with fever. "Why didn't you say you were ill?"

"It caught me by surprise, too. I thought since it had been months... Malaria," he said, when she shook her head, not comprehending. "It will p-pass in a few hours. If you could help me get to the door."

"You wouldn't make it a quarter of a mile before you drove off the road and killed yourself, and I don't need that on my conscience. Come lie down. Pilot," she snapped, when her dog decided it was playtime and jumped against Gabriel. "Get down."

"This is unnecessary," Gabriel muttered, trying to resist her. "You don't need this inconvenience."

Ignoring him and slipping an arm around his waist, she awkwardly made her way toward the couch. Once there she unceremoniously nudged him onto it. "We're going to have to get you out of some of those wet clothes. Get you warm. Stay put and I'll get some blankets."

She raced back to her bedroom and snatched up the throw on the foot of her bed, then grabbed another heavier blanket from the closet. When she returned to the living room, she found Gabriel still where she'd left him, huddled in almost a fetal position and shaking uncontrollably. He seemed barely aware of her as she adjusted the sofa pillows on one end of the couch and spread the covers over the other end. But when she stooped to remove his shoes and lift his legs onto the cushions, he muttered in protest.

"Lisa . . . you should have l-let me l-leave."

"Life is full of 'should haves'," she replied, ignoring the strange thrill she'd felt hearing her name roll off his tongue. "You're here and that's that." Lisa took off his soaked socks, as well, then wrapped the first blanket around the lower part of his body. "I can't tell if you're wet from the rain or fever," she said, sliding her hands over his chest before beginning to undo his shirt buttons. "Can you help me get this off?"

He tried but it took forever because he couldn't maintain any control over his hands. Finally, however, they succeeded in their task. It was then that Lisa noticed his chest and the stark delination of rib bones beneath the sparest amount of flesh. She couldn't hide the sound of dismay that rose from deep within her. "My God, when was the last time you ate a decent meal?"

Gabriel's lips compressed into what was closer to a grimace than a smile. "A full spirit is of greater value than a full stomach,'' he replied through chattering teeth.

"Is that so? And where did you learn that pearl of wisdom?''

"St. Jude's.''

"Is that a hospital?''

"Hospital . . . n-no. St. Jude's was the mission where I recuperated.''

Three

_____

Lisa sprang upright in bed. Though it took her a few seconds, she soon realized that the sound she'd heard wasn't Gabriel once again shivering or tossing restlessly in his sleep, but her radio alarm clock telling her it was time to get up.

Already? Rubbing her face with her hands, she moaned. She had no idea what time she finally climbed into bed, but what sleep she did get hadn't revitalized her enough to where she was ready to deal with twenty-nine highly energized sixth graders. Nor was she anywhere near prepared to face Marie Thomas. As fond as she was of her friend and fellow teacher, she wasn't up to the hard sell she would inevitably receive to join in on that "fun" shopping-spree weekend in Knoxville that Marie had been talking about all week. And, she thought with a silent groan, she definitely wasn't looking forward to another parent-teacher consultation with

Jimmy Nolan's stepmother. Thank goodness it was Friday; at least she would have the weekend to recuperate from the emotional upheaval of last night.

As she tugged the sliding lace strap of her negligee to where it belonged on her shoulder, she wondered how Gabriel had fared the rest of the night. She hadn't left him until he'd slipped into a deep exhausted sleep. Considering how long the progressive bout of chills, fever and sweats had lasted, she wouldn't be surprised if she was going to have trouble rousing him.

She reached over and turned off her radio, which had Pilot rising from the blue-and-mauve throw rug beside the bed. Except for the noisy yawn he made while stretching, it seemed quiet in the house; but since she'd closed her door when she'd finally retreated to her own room, she couldn't be sure. At any rate, if she was going to follow through with her plan to prepare Gabriel a decent breakfast before sending him on his way and leaving for school, she needed to get moving.

Stifling a yawn, she slid out of bed. At least she would finally have something interesting to add to the general conversation when she joined Marie and some of the other teachers in the dining room for lunch. Normally her recitations about sanding and revarnishing hardwood floors, painting rooms or clearing more of the overgrowth of brush on her property made Marie tease her about living a "cloistered life-style." Lisa didn't think her life was all that boring; it simply wasn't her nature to be as socially adventurous as Marie. But, Lisa thought with an impish smile, even Marie had never had someone like Gabriel Ballesteros show up on her doorstep.

Still, Lisa knew she wouldn't tell her friend everything about last night. She couldn't reveal to anyone how Gabriel and Jon were connected, and she definitely wouldn't confess her most intimate thoughts of how the longer she'd ministered to Gabriel—determinedly holding the covers over him while he shivered, then bathing his sweat-slick body when he turned feverish—the stronger the feeling grew that it wouldn't be easy to forget him. Yet the truth of it was as undeniable as the first rays of sunlight spearing around the edges of her window shades.

What she needed, she told herself with a new surge of practicality, was a brisk shower to wash away the fanciful nonsense cluttering her mind like cobwebs. Thank goodness she'd had the foresight to wash her hair last night between sojourns at Gabriel's side. Just drying it would have used up a full half hour she couldn't spare this morning.

As Pilot pressed against her leg to remind her of his presence, she leaned over to give him his morning scratch behind both ears. "I'd better let you outside, too, hadn't I?" she murmured affectionately. "We'll have to be quiet, though—and no barking at squirrels until later."

Side by side they shuffled to the door and Lisa swung it open, only to have her first step into the hall bring her face-to-face with Gabriel. Though there wasn't even time to gasp in surprise, she managed to place a hand against his chest to keep herself from barreling into him. At the same time he, too, moved defensively, catching her by her waist to steady them both.

For a few heart-thumping seconds, they stared at one another in mute wonder. At least, that was what Lisa told herself it was in the beginning, because she was truly astonished he'd awakened this early and appeared no worse for wear despite all he'd been through the previous night. But as she grew aware of the heat his hands generated, wonder grew into something far less innocent.

Her silk gown was no protection against his burning touch, which spread through her body like a flash fire, obliterating every thought from her mind except one. For the first time in years she wanted to be held again. But not held by just anyone, and not just held; she wanted this man's arms around her, and she wanted to be swept away in the tide of mindless passion *he'd* inspired.

Beneath her fingers, his heartbeat grew stronger, quickened. His pectoral muscles turned hot and hard with tensile strength. She didn't need the words to know that he, too, was sensitive to the mysterious chemistry churning between them, and it only proved to Lisa that last night hadn't been a fluke. It wasn't the storm, the lateness of the hour or any of the other dozen excuses she'd tried to fabricate in order to explain away her confusing and disturbing attraction to him. Yet, even as she struggled to remind herself she wanted no part of this, she was profoundly aware that no matter what happened or whether they put inches or miles between them, this indefinable undeniable feeling wouldn't go away.

Then he subtly tightened his hold. Lisa sucked fresh air into her lungs.

That urge to kiss her was back in his eyes, stronger than before, and the part of her that was a coward wished he would just do it. At least then the decision would have been out of her hands. But it was clear he wanted her to make the first move, let him know it was what she really wanted. That challenge, his willful restraint, was all she needed to remind her she was on the brink of behaving rashly, perhaps even dangerously.

Just because he'd rekindled her feminine libido didn't mean she should abandon all common sense. They were still little more than strangers, and from the messages that had been arcing between them, it was highly unlikely things would have stopped with only a kiss. The recklessness and widespread ramifications of such an impulsive decision notwithstanding, Lisa knew she was in no condition to become emotionally involved with anyone right now—particularly not someone whose mere presence kept resurrecting painful memories of Jon. And it would have to be an emotional involvement; she'd never been able to overcome her aversion to one-night stands.

Gabriel must have seen the withdrawal in her eyes, because he was the first one to move, slowly releasing her. "I startled you."

His voice sounded thick—from sleep or desire? Lisa shook her head, but only to stop the stubborn one-track route her thoughts were taking. "I'm just trying to wake up, that's all."

"Yes, your eyes still look heavy with sleep. It's very provocative."

Sweet sharp pleasure speared through Lisa leaving her body tingling and spawning an aching sensation in her womb and her breasts. Suddenly remembering her lace-and-silk gown was hardly respectable attire for entertaining a houseguest, she crossed her arms in front of her. She was also grateful when Pilot insinuated himself between them, demanding attention.

"How do you feel this morning?" she asked self-consciously, as Gabriel scowled at her dog.

"Weak, which is normal after these attacks, but otherwise better. I'm grateful to you for your hospitality and...faith."

"Faith?"

"You didn't have to put up with me."

"I don't see that I had much choice," she told him, allowing the shadow of a smile, wry though it was, to curve her lips.

"You could have telephoned the police."

Her answering look was rife with surprise. Not only hadn't she considered that, she wondered how he could suggest it. "Wouldn't that have been...inconvenient for you?"

"It would depend on what questions they asked."

His calmness confused her and his vague responses were beginning to grate on her nerves. Was she doomed to be attracted only to men who liked to keep secrets? "Do you have the necessary documentation to be in the States?"

"Of course."

"Do you think the police have a file on you?"

"I can't imagine why they would."

Lisa purged her breath in a swoosh and impatiently raked her hair back from her face. "You're a friend of Jon's all right. The two of you could have written the book on how to give broad but nebulous answers."

She made an attempt to step around him, but he reached out to block her. The heat from his arm, a hairbreadth away from her breasts, froze her in place.

"Lisa, a moment, please. Give me another chance."

The intensity with which he spoke had her raising her head to search his face. What kind of chance? her heart cried. One minute he was calling her provocative and the next he was trying to avoid giving her any information about himself. What did he want from her?

"Old habits," he murmured, reminding her of what he'd said the night before. "I'll tell you what you want to know—perhaps over a cup of your excellent coffee? But first—" His smile was apologetic "—nature calls."

Lisa ducked her head and murmured that she needed to let Pilot out for exactly that reason. Excusing herself and practically hugging the wall, she slipped by him.

It was twenty minutes later when she joined him in the kitchen. The coffee she'd set to perk after letting Pilot out was done, and Gabriel was standing by the bay window in the dinette sipping on a mug of the steaming brew. He'd found the shirt she'd rinsed out and pressed, but now he wore it more casually, rolling up the sleeves and leaving the top two buttons open. Despite his weakened state the white cotton emphasized his dramatic dark coloring, and she found the dusting of black hair on his forearms and at his throat enormously sexy.

"It'll only take a few minutes to get breakfast," she said, adopting the polite but impersonal attitude she'd decided would be the safest way to deal with him.

Turning, Gabriel did a slow thorough survey of her, though Lisa thought the dress she'd chosen for today was hardly worth a second look. She resisted the impulse to glance down at the simple shirtwaist herself. At least the aqua-green shade suited her blond coloring, and the slim skirt flattered her figure. Still, it was plain; the green-and-yellow print scarf she'd draped artfully around her shoulders was the best she could do to dress it up.

"I'm in no hurry," Gabriel told her, before spreading his arms to indicate the shirt. "Thank you for this. What's packed in my suitcase probably looks worse than this did when you took it off me."

"You're quite welcome." She sounded disgustingly prim, but being reminded of how it had felt to undress him wasn't something she needed right now. She moistened her lips. "Do you like ham? There's a family-owned market in town that smokes their own, and I guarantee it'll make your mouth water."

"Whatever you choose to prepare for yourself will be fine."

"The ham then, and biscuits with honey, courtesy of Bentonville's own bees. You can't leave here without having tasted it, either." Grateful her back was to him, Lisa winced. She couldn't have been more blunt if she'd asked whether he needed directions to the nearest interstate highway.

With an inward sigh, she poured herself a mug of coffee. It was too hot to take more than a sip, but the way her nerves seemed determined to stay tied in knots when she was around this man, anything was a help.

"Have you lived here long?"

He had to be part cat, Lisa thought when she shot a glance over her shoulder and found that Gabriel had moved closer to watch her work and was now leaning over the far side of the counter. The way he could do that without her having heard him unnerved her. "Only since last summer. I suppose it shows," she added dryly, drawing the electric skillet from a cabinet and connecting the plug with the pan, then inserting the other end into the wall socket. "I know there's a lot left to do, but during the school year I only have the weekends to make any noticeable progress."

"What you've accomplished so far looks wonderful."

"Thank you. I like it. This used to be a mom-and-pop operation."

"I beg your pardon?"

"This was a motel owned and operated by an elderly couple. We're only a few miles away from Gatlinburg and, come winter, the whole area turns into a mecca for skiers. The Great Smokies aren't exactly the Alps, but people make do. In the summer we have a fair number of honeymooners and hikers. I have four cottages, such as they are, on twelve acres, and I'm hoping to eventually get them renovated and then reopen for business."

"That's a sizable undertaking."

"True, but then again I'm not going anywhere." Lisa added margarine to the heated skillet and the sizzling became a comfort of sorts, filling in the sudden silence that followed her comment.

"Weren't you happy in Alexandria?" Gabriel asked at last.

Lisa nearly dropped the roll of canned biscuits and the ham she'd just taken out of the refrigerator. Clutching them to her chest, she spun around. "How do you know I'm from Alexandria?"

Glancing away, he shrugged. "Jon mentioned it. That's where I looked for you first."

"Oh."

"He also told me that you were born in West Virginia to older parents, that they died when you were barely out of college, and that you had no siblings. I suppose you felt there were no longer any ties to keep you there?"

It cost Lisa to distribute the biscuits patiently over a cookie sheet, when what she really wanted to do was scream. What right had Jon had to tell anyone about her when he kept almost everything about himself a secret?

"It was something like that," she managed reluctantly. "As he said, I'm from West Virginia—a country girl. The only reason I'd moved to Alexandria in the first place was to get a good job. But being so close to the city, the inevitable reminder of the government and people that tried to keep the truth about my husband from me ... I had to get away." After placing the biscuits in the oven, she sliced the ham and set it in the skillet. "What about you? Do you have family back in Argentina?"

"No, like you there's no one."

"How long are you planning on staying in the States?"

"Permanently."

Surprised, Lisa risked shooting another quick glance his way. "Because you were in the same type of busines Jon was and your cover has been blown?"

"Along with my good looks, eh?"

Lisa shut her eyes briefly. "I'm sorry. That was a terrible choice of words."

"It doesn't matter. The point is there's nothing to go back to, while here in America ... anything is possible."

His raspy voice, the way he enunciated each word so that it became a sensual caress, made the fine hairs on Lisa's arms rise. She ducked her head, determined he should not see how easily he was getting behind her defenses. "Do you mind if I ask you what your official occupation was?"

"Officially and unofficially it was one and the same. I was a liaison to the American ambassador to Argentina."

As hard as she tried, Lisa couldn't repress a cynical smile. "That sounds appropriately harmless."

"It often was," he replied pleasantly. "And tedious. I won't miss the clerical work at least."

"I'll bet." She could tell he was enjoying himself and, annoyed, she decided to scramble the eggs she'd taken from the refrigerator without asking him for his preference. "How did you and Jon meet?"

"The ambassador asked me to pick him up at the airport one day."

"And ultimately he convinced you to work with him?"

Gabriel shook his head at her unmistakable disapproval. "Jon never had to coerce me to help him. I did whatever I did because I wanted to."

Lisa paused in reaching for the silverware. His tone asked for her understanding and, heaven help her, she found herself wanting to give him the benefit of the doubt. "Jon was an extremely charismatic man. I understand perfectly." Wanting to change the subject, she asked, "Where did you contract malaria? I thought it was a tropical or subtropical disease."

"It is. I caught it years ago on a flight from Brazil to Columbia. The charter plane I was in went down in the Amazon and it was several days before we were found."

"Good Lord," Lisa said, staring at him in amazement. "You *have* lived an adventurous life. But if you contracted it years ago, why did you have a relapse last night?"

"Malaria is often recurrent. That was the first attack I've experienced in a long time. I would imagine it was my fatigue and getting chilled that brought it on."

It sounded reasonable, Lisa thought, setting the cozy linen-covered table by the bay window. Secretly wishing she'd had time to go out back and pluck a stalk or two of her orange bearded irises to complement the white-and-blue decor, she invited Gabriel to sit down. "You still don't look as though you're feeling all that terrific." When he took the seat that allowed him to observe her, as well as admire the outdoor scenery, she continued, "Would you mind if I asked you about something you said last night?"

"*Por favor,* you may ask anything you wish," he told her smoothly, looking more amused than concerned.

Lisa didn't have to wonder why. Whether he would answer her question or not—and truthfully or not—was something only he would decide. "Don't worry," she assured him dryly. "I'm not about to ask you to divulge any state secrets. But you said you'd recuperated in a mission—St. Jude's I think you called it. I was wondering, was that the extenuating circumstance that kept you from delivering my husband's message sooner?"

"*Sí.* I required . . . several operations."

"Your leg still seems to be giving you difficulty."

Gabriel's smile, though slight, transformed his face into near handsomeness and had Lisa's pulse doing crazy things. "Not at all," he replied wryly. "The leg had healed. I merely had a minor mishap outside of your Dulles airport. A child was about to have an encounter with one of your notoriously aggressive taxicabs and I intervened."

Nothing else he might have said could have disarmed her more completely. He'd risked his own life for a child. That wasn't the action of a man who had ice in his veins—which she had come to believe was what Jon must have possessed to do what he'd done to her. Gabriel was a simpler man with a good heart. His past, whatever he'd been or done had left him with haunted memories; she could see how they shadowed his good eye. What right did she have to add to his misery?

Relaxing for the first time since she'd answered the phone the night before, Lisa quickly finished preparing their breakfast and then set a food-laden platter before her guest. His deep indrawn breath and subsequent sigh of pleasure were reward enough, but when he looked up to smile at her, she felt something far more effervescent bubble within her.

"If you fed Jon this way, it's a wonder he managed to keep in the shape he did."

Lisa's own smile wavered and she stepped away to get her plate and refill their coffee mugs. "We...we weren't married long enough for him to have worried about that."

As she sat, she was aware that Gabriel had put down his fork and was watching her. His expression was troubled. "Would you allow me a personal question?" he asked huskily.

"Considering all that I've asked you, it would only be fair."

"You seem to harbor mixed feelings about your marriage. Do you regret having fallen in love with Jon?"

Caught in the hypnotic power of his gaze, Lisa couldn't evade the truth. "Sometimes." The confession hurt so much she was immediately compelled to shake her head in rejection. "No, not regret exactly. But I've spent the past three years in such emotional turmoil. There are so many questions I'll never have answers to—questions I *need* answers to—and sometimes it makes me want to scream. At him. At God. At everyone."

Dropping her head back, she gazed up at the ceiling and expelled a grief-filled breath. "And then I remember how I felt when I was with him. No one ever made me feel more alive, more beautiful or cherished. He brought me passion that most women probably only dream of knowing. I would have done *anything* for him."

"A love that strong would be capable of forgiving him his deceit."

Dabbing away the wetness that threatened to spill over her lashes with the backs of her index fingers, Lisa's answering look was dubious. "You think so? I think that if by some miracle he did walk back into my life... Oh, I would be glad for him, of course. But I don't think I would allow myself to get caught up in him again. It was simply too much."

"So you intend to protect yourself from passion by withdrawing from life?"

"I haven't withdrawn," she protested, not wanting anyone to find flaws in her carefully constructed method of self-preservation. "I teach, I have friends and this," she said, gesturing to encompass her house and land.

"I was referring to the more intimate variety of passion. The kind between a man and woman. The kind that knows no boundaries and can barely be sated before it begins to throb again. The kind of passion that reduces the rest of the universe to a handful of glittering stardust.''

If anyone else, even a friend, had said that to her, Lisa would have primly informed them that her private life wasn't any of their business. But because Gabriel had come so close to describing what she'd lost, she answered with brutal honesty.

''I don't ever want to experience passion again. At least not the intense kind, that all-consuming variety. And to be perfectly honest, I haven't felt ready to even consider dating, so I don't see that I have to worry about it.''

There didn't seem to be much more to say after that, and for several minutes both Lisa and Gabriel concentrated on their meal. He made several impeccably polite comments about the food and she accepted them with the formality of a hostess at a State Department dinner. Yet there was no denying the underlying pleasure she felt sharing breakfast with him. She missed cooking for someone other than herself, missed having someone to show the irises and pansies blooming in the rock garden, and even though she shifted to keep it from happening again, she missed having a strong masculine knee brush lightly against her thigh under the table.

''What time do you have to be at your school?'' Gabriel asked, finally pushing away his thoroughly cleaned plate.

As he rose to refill his coffee mug, Lisa smiled inwardly. It pleased her that he felt comfortable enough to help himself. ''In about fifty minutes, but it's only a fifteen-minute drive, so there's no rush.'' When he surprised her further by bringing the pot to refill her mug, she murmured bemused thanks before asking, "What about you?"

"I have no scheduled appointments."

"No, I meant, where are you headed next?"

"I have no idea." Having replaced the pot on the burner, he returned to his seat. His movements stirred the air and made Lisa notice how crisp and attractive her bath soap smelled on him. "I suppose I should find a hotel and sleep off this jet lag. After that...who knows."

"You mean you haven't decided what you're going to do?"

"I'm fairly certain I'll resist offering my services as liaison to any Argentinean embassy or consulate," he said wryly.

"You think that's funny?" As soon as the words were out, Lisa ducked her head and stared at her plate. She'd had no business saying that, of course, but his words had conjured up scenes of violence, more death.

Just as he'd done the previous night, Gabriel reached out to her, only to once again withdraw. "I'm sorry. I was only trying to make light of what appears to be a considerable, though not impossible, dilemma for me. Still, I have my health and, despite what my current condition might suggest, two strong arms."

"How are you at carpentry?" Lisa asked impulsively, before she could remind herself of all the reasons why she shouldn't.

"I beg your pardon?"

The way he lifted his stark right eyebrow made her feel more than a little foolish. "Never mind. It's probably a silly idea. At any rate, I doubt it's something a liaison to the Argentinean ambassador would be interested in."

"Believe me, after spending the better part of three years sleeping on cots made of hay and eating out of donated dishes, my pride has learned not to get in the way of survival. Precisely what were you about to suggest?"

"A temporary job of sorts," she replied, unable to meet his steady gaze except for fleeting glances. "And a roof over your head. You need the time to rest for a few days and then to decide what you want to do with your future. I . . . I need someone to help me with the heavier renovation work."

"You want me to stay here? With you?" he asked slowly.

"Well, actually, what I had in mind was . . . that is, one of the cottages is in fairly good shape. It shouldn't take more than a good dusting and vacuuming and some new curtains to make it inhabitable. There's already a good bed in there and some other furniture I moved out of here when I brought my own things."

His guarded expression didn't give away any of his feelings, but there was something about his quiet rigidity that made Lisa suddenly realize she'd made a serious mistake. Exactly what it was, however, she wasn't sure.

"Do you realize what you're suggesting?" he asked when the silence had grown to an almost palpable throb.

Lisa nearly gulped when she heard the anger vibrating in his voice. "I only wanted to help."

"Why?"

"Because you need a place to stay."

"Isn't that the purpose of hotels?"

"In the long run they can be expensive."

"I'm not destitute," he muttered, crushing his napkin in his hand and flinging it on his plate. "And furthermore you don't know me well enough to make such an offer."

"I wouldn't know much about a handyman I hired, either."

"The handyman wouldn't be living with you."

"Neither will you!" Lisa sprang to her feet, as confused by his sudden strange behavior as she was angered by it. "I don't know what your problem is, but you're obviously right, it was a bad idea. Let's forget it." She began collecting the dishes, too upset to care that her rough handling was testing their durability.

"We won't 'forget it,'" he snapped, rising and following her to the sink. "Not until you understand the trouble you could've been inviting. My God, woman, have you no sense of self-preservation? What do you know about me?"

Seeing the fury in his gaze, Lisa nearly dropped the dishes she was lowering into the sink and, turning completely, reached behind her to grip the counter. "You're Jon's friend."

"So I say. That's not enough!"

"Well, what was I supposed to do—check your pockets last night and verify your credentials? I'm sorry it's a belated thought, but last night I was too concerned about your health."

"Why me?" Gabriel insisted, ignoring what she'd said and placing his hands on either side of the counter, boxing her in.

"Because I think—I *know*—I could trust you."

He swore softly. "You're wrong! Don't your realize my staying would only prompt the inevitable?"

Painfully aware that he'd struck dead center on the truth, Lisa couldn't bring herself to meet his fierce gaze and kept her eyes on the pulse beating rapidly at the base of his throat. "It needn't happen."

Shifting suddenly, Gabriel took hold of Lisa's waist and drew her tightly against him. "Who's going to stop it? Which one of us is strong enough? You think I don't feel what's happening between us? You think I can't see the bewilderment and passion in your eyes?"

As his breath caressed her lips and his body betrayed his heightened arousal to her, Lisa felt her own body's reaction and panic raced along with her blood. "Gabriel—don't. Please."

"Why not? It's been between us from the moment you opened your door to me."

"No."

"Yes!" He lowered his head. *"Yes,"* he rasped, taking full possession of her lips.

To Lisa it was like being roused from a long deep sleep. His tongue unhesitatingly thrust into her mouth. His hands crushed her to his lean hungry body. At first she resisted the shock to her nervous system. Instinct told her she didn't want to feel—not this hot, not this good. Feeling, some corner of her consciousness warned, was going to hurt, badly. Yet Gabriel Ballesteros kissed like a man who'd been starving for the chance.

Urgent. His lips moved urgently over hers, tasting, claiming, his tongue probing and, when she resisted him, demanding. He might as well have been stripping her—Lisa felt his possession completely. And yet there was no violence, only stomach-wrenching need that had her moaning because she discovered she was far more vulnerable to it than anything else.

"Oh, please," she cried, breaking the kiss and thrusting her head back to suck sweet fresh air into her lungs. "Don't do this. I don't want it."

"Yes, you do." His hands, fingers splayed to encompass her hips, stroked, explored. His mouth, seeking another kiss, satisfied itself with the soft skin along her arching throat.

"I promised myself never again," she moaned, as he tasted her, bit lightly at her earlobe.

"Forever is a long time, *mi deseo.*"

My desire. As he captured her lips again, the translation reached through the walls of her resistence like a shattering cry through deathly silence. For three years she had rejected with no difficulty the advances of men who thought they could "ease her widow's grieving," even an awkward pass from her former next-door neighbor. But she wasn't strong enough to resist a man who had a unique talent for continually touching her heart as Gabriel did. She wasn't hardened enough to remain immune to the caresses of a man who seemed to understand exactly how to touch her to make her most vulnerable to him. Still, she didn't consciously make a decision; her body did it for her.

Her fingers uncurled from the tight fists pressed against his chest and sought more of him at the opened V of his shirt. Her mouth stopped trying to evade his kisses but instigated one of its own. Her body, previously frozen in shock, melted against his.

"Lisa..." His raw sensual whisper brought a feverish flush to her face, just as his kisses had. He brushed his lips across her cheek, to her forehead, and again down the length of her throat. "So soft. So gentle. And these eyes—my little dove's eyes," he groaned, awarding poignant kisses to each closed lid.

Lisa's heartbeat faltered. Her breath locked in her throat, blocking a gasp of shock and disbelief. *No,* she screamed inwardly. "No!" came the wail she forced up through her frozen vocal chords.

"Lisa...?" In his aroused state, Gabriel was slow to pick up on what was wrong; but when he felt the change in her, saw the expression on her face, his own became veiled and watchful. "What is it?"

"Stop it!" she screamed, twisting away from him, then slapping at the hands that tried to hold her. "Stop pretending. *Lying.* No one but Jon ever said that about my eyes. No one else knew he did!"

Gabriel remained completely, guiltily silent.

She almost laughed; it was too bizarre, too unreal. She had to be losing her mind. Then she saw the resignation in his eye and she pressed her clasped hands to her trembling lips. "Oh, God... it is you. It's *you.*"

Four

He should have known he wouldn't be able to pull off the plan. Not with Lisa. Not once he'd touched her.

He stood outside on the back patio and sucked the crisp mountain air deep into his lungs, but was otherwise oblivious to the bucolic scenery he'd admired earlier. How could he dwell on the majesty of towering hardwood trees and the charm of wild azaleas and laurel blooming behind Lisa's painstakingly cultivated flower beds, when the image of her sweet face—at first shocked, then hurt and furious—kept haunting him?

Ah, Lisa, I was only trying to spare you.

But because he couldn't keep his mouth shut and his hands to himself, he'd ruined things. For good this time. She felt betrayed all over again; he knew it as surely as he'd accepted that staying away had been impossible, and heaven knows how hard he'd tried to do that. He'd lost her, and the knowledge was spawning a

pain as terrible as any he'd suffered these past three
years.

She wasn't going to be able to see past his deceit and
comprehend why he'd been compelled to do what he'd
done; why he hadn't attempted to contact her after all
this time; but mostly why he'd kept so much of himself
a secret even though she'd been his wife. His work, his
choices, had shut her out. What woman could get past
the reality of that? All he could do was wait and try not
to think about what was going on inside the house.

It was her tears that had driven him out here, even
though he'd anticipated them, knew she would need the
chance to purge the shock and hurt. He'd been trying to
give her that space when he let her run away to the bedroom, resigning himself to pacing the length and
breadth of the living room. But the sobs that had
echoed down the hall had been more heart-wrenching
than what he'd heard in his worst nightmares; they'd
proved to be too much, affecting him like razor-sharp
daggers piercing his chest, his head, his very soul.

Another minute of that relentless keening and he
wouldn't have been able to stop himself. He would have
broken down the bedroom door she'd locked to keep
him out. But then what? he'd asked himself with the last
corner of rational intelligence he possessed. She wasn't
ready to let him explain. She certainly wouldn't let him
hold her; hell would be more likely to grow lilies first.

So he was waiting, and thinking, and—wouldn't this
give Sennett a good laugh?—praying.

Perhaps Oscar had been right, he thought, shutting
his eyes tightly against a new surge of anguish. The old
dinosaur had warned him it was too late, that too much
time had gone by for him to come back and that he
might as well resign himself to becoming a useful mem-

ber of "the family." At best, the aging physician-turned-missionary had warned, this was an invitation for havoc, at worst, catastrophe.

All his reasons had been feasible, though demoralizing. What if Lisa had remarried? What if she panicked and phoned the police, forcing Gabriel to face the prospect of the wrong people finding out he was still alive? But none of those well-intended suppositions had carried enough weight to change Gabriel's mind once he'd settled on a course of action.

He'd needed to know that Lisa was alive, safe, well. There had never been a day in the past three years—at least not after he'd regained consciousness—that she hadn't been in the forefront of his mind. There hadn't been a night when the memories of their lovemaking hadn't both saved and tormented him. He'd reached a point where, despite his aversion to what he faced every time he looked in a mirror, he'd known he had to risk seeing her just once more. Gone were the fantasies he'd entertained about getting back into her life; reality was cold, and he would rather face her fury than be subjected to her pity.

He'd needed some peace of mind. To know she was all right—that had been and still was his sincerest intention.

But he should have been more honest with himself when it came to dealing with his passion. He should have known he wouldn't be able to keep his hands off her.

Just thinking about those few precious seconds when he'd abandoned all common sense and let need overcome his honorable motives made the next breath he exhaled hiss sharply. It had been everything he'd dreamed in his most vivid fantasies. She'd tasted sweeter than he'd remembered, and her response—once he'd broken through her defenses—had been that same uninhibited sensuality that had made her an obsession to him in the first place. Heaven save his worthless soul; another few seconds and he would have carried her to the bedroom to slake the hunger that had slowly been destroying him.

The mere pleasure of looking at her last night had been worth what it cost him to get back into the country. Holding her, kissing her, had salvaged his sanity faster than that first shot of morphine Oscar had given him when those villagers had hauled his near-dead carcass into Doc's dismal excuse for a clinic. No one had ever affected him as Lisa did.

And she was every bit as lovely as he remembered. Lovelier, despite the obvious effects his purported death and Sennett's big mouth had had on her. Granted, he'd seen children who weighed more than she did these days, but he didn't have to look in a mirror to see he himself practically resembled a survivor of a POW camp. No matter, it was her eyes he loved to focus on, anyway, and what was behind them. What he'd seen in their depths last night had made his heart ache with the same unbearable longing he'd felt the first time he'd seen her.

Lisa's eyes had always been his salvation. When he'd met her, he had been on a collision course with his own mortality, thanks to his restless rootless personality and dangerous occupation. He knew it, knew the odds were against his reaching a ripe old age, but until then he hadn't cared. Like his soldier-father who'd died in a Far East jungle, he'd been born with the desire to live life to the fullest, and whatever or wherever it took him to achieve that suited him fine.

Then, one lazy Saturday afternoon while killing a few hours before a scheduled appointment with Sennett, he'd wandered through the street fair near his apartment and spotted her. It had been unbelievable, corny, almost enough to give him second thoughts about his long-neglected religion. His attention was caught by a veil of tawny waist-length hair cascading over a rack of used books. The body that went with the hair was barely average in height and nymph-slender. He remembered thinking she wasn't exactly the type he was normally drawn to.

Yet something about the self-contained preoccupied quality of the young woman had held his interest. It was as if she was truly fascinated with those dusty old books to the point where she was oblivious to the crush of people milling around her, the heavy clouds swiftly covering the sun and threatening a chilling rain, or the elderly shopkeeper who was gazing at her with hopefulness and approval. The urge to see her face became a need that had him pushing through the crowd and heading straight for her.

To this day he didn't understand what had happened after that. If someone had told him that lightning had struck the ground beside him and short-circuited the connection between his head and heart, he would have accepted that as a perfectly reasonable explanation; clearly fate had decided his time had come. When she turned to go into the store, excited with some find, they came face-to-face and he was caught in a bittersweet web of desire, enchantment—love. Yes, from the beginning, though he'd long been a stranger to the emotion, there had been stirrings of love.

Something about her face had made him think of forbidden fruit. It was her purity, that untainted quality she possessed, which he'd seen even as he watched her in the throes of orgasm. He could make her eyes dark with passion, and yet serenity always shimmered in their depths. His Lisa, he soon learned, possessed the kind of soul he hadn't even known as a boy.

The moment he recognized that, saw it in her pale honest face, in her sweet enchanting smile, he knew if he had an ounce of decency, he would walk away from her. He'd barely begun to skim beneath the first layers of who and what she was, but he'd already understood she deserved better than him. Yet one look into those gentle gray eyes and, God forgive him, he'd become a selfish bastard, a regular Barabbas reaching for life with the lust of a survivor.

He'd known from the first that she was no match for him; a young woman barely out of college, maybe not a virgin, but compared to him an innocent. Still he wanted her. Even his body craved to possess her sylph-like form, his soul ached for its first brush with real honesty. Had he believed that some of it might rub off on him? Had his presumptuousness been so great that he'd thought his sins could be discounted through her?

He didn't allow himself to dwell on the answers. Instead he seduced her, using all the charm and sensuality he possessed, knowing she would be as helpless to resist him as she was fascinated by the unknown commodity he represented.

Even then he should have seen what he'd done and left her in her safer world. But it was already too late.

He'd become as caught up as she was in the surreal dream they'd created in each other's arms. Possession made him greedy, obsession made him afraid of losing her; and so he married her, keeping the truth of who and what he really was a secret. He'd meant it as protection for her—so that she wouldn't be exposed to the ugliness he knew was an inevitable part of his business—and for him, to safeguard himself against losing the most cherished discovery he'd made in his life.

And now he was about to lose her for yet a second and final time. Not only because of his deceit, but because in a matter of hours she'd already begun to fall in love with the wounded redeemable Gabriel Ballesteros. He should be laughing at the irony of it all, but it hurt too much.

The sound of Pilot's running yanked him out of his brooding. He watched the big-boned dog race for him, ears flat and eyes slitted like a pup knowing it was about to be embraced and coddled. He twisted his lips into a weary smile, amused at the thought of how Lisa had tamed even this great beast. Then, as he began to lean down to offer a pat, the mutt raced past him.

He turned to find Lisa stooping in the doorway soothing the great curl of fur that hunkered and squirmed at her feet. After placating Pilot with a generous rubbing, she rose and focused, he noted bitterly, on the clay swan resting on the middle of the picnic table rather than on him.

"I need answers," she stated, her normally smooth voice ravaged from her violent weeping.

Without waiting for a reply, she retreated into the house. He followed her and the dog inside, wishing he could do something to ease the tension and pain he saw had her hugging her arms around herself and ducking her head into her shoulders like a terrified turtle that suddenly found itself on the freeway. Her eyes were red and swollen, and clearly embarrassed, she avoided his attempt to make eye contact. It was also obvious she didn't want him to get too close to her, though that didn't stop his need to try. When he rounded the couch, however, she slipped behind the high-backed chair; when he followed, she went behind the one he'd sat in last night. Finally, as she edged toward the fireplace, he found himself wondering if she really wanted to pick up one of those brass-handled fire irons, and could she bring herself to use it on him. He became resigned to staying put. As if content with his decision, Pilot settled on the braided rug in the center of the room.

"Would you like me to call someone for you?" He stroked the back of the easy chair the way he used to caress her hair when she lay in his arms after they'd made love. "Under the circumstances, I don't think you're in any condition to teach today."

"I already took care of it."

The shell-shocked quality of her voice had a band of cold steel gripping his heart, and he took a deep controlled breath, not unlike those he used when meditating. He knew she was still too close to hysteria's edge for him to risk allowing even a mild hint of his real feelings to show. "Will it create problems for you—their having to find a replacement on such short notice?"

That earned him a direct and hardly reassuring look. "It doesn't concern you."

As he dug his fingers into the chair's soft upholstery, he reminded himself that if he'd learned one thing from the months he'd spent flat on his back, it was that people could endure more than they thought themselves capable of, even him. "Perhaps you no longer feel I have a right to be concerned—and perhaps I don't," he said quietly. "Nevertheless, I am."

Nerves had her lacing and twisting her fingers, but when she found herself fidgeting with her wedding band, she thrust her hands behind her back and forced herself to meet his solemn scrutiny. "I don't want to talk about me, I want you to..." Her voice broke, and he had to steel himself against yet another urge to go to her.

"Go ahead and ask, *querida,*" he prompted gently. "You have every right."

A tear slipped past her lashes and raced down her cheek. Ruthlessly she brushed it away. *"Why?"* she whispered at last.

He didn't pretend to need any clarification. "To protect you."

"Please," she scoffed. "No more lies. I'm not the naive fool you once knew."

"It's the truth." His tone was more harsh than he'd intended, but her desecration of the love they'd shared was pushing him toward his own edge. "And you were never a fool."

"Well—" she had to swallow to find her voice "—I still don't believe you."

"No. Why should you? If our positions were reversed I, too, would have been skeptical."

"Stop it," she moaned, bending from the waist as if she were in physical agony. "Stop using that accent and pretending to be *him.* The game is over. You're Jonathan Howard!"

"As far as the world outside this house is concerned, Jon Howard is dead, Lisa, and after today you'd do well to go back to believing that yourself. As for my accent—" his shrug was a gesture of weariness more than indifference "—it's become second nature to me, since Spanish is practically all I've spoken for the past three years." Seeing she was accepting that much, he risked taking a step toward her. "Hate me if you must, *querida,* but for your own sake accept that."

Lisa's wide-eyed gaze mirrored startled thoughts. "For my sake... Are you saying I could be in danger?"

Not if he could help it. He would turn himself over to either ally or enemy before he let anyone harm her, but he knew she was in no frame of mind to hear declarations like that. "No. At least not as long as you don't hold a press conference to announce that yet another Lazarus has risen from the grave." That made her wince and he extended a hand toward her. "Lisa, if there had been any other way—"

"Don't touch me," she warned, hugging herself again. "I'm not interested in your apology. I only want to know why? Why did you allow me to believe you were dead? Why did you take so long to come back and then pretend to be... to make me wonder if I was..."

He narrowed his eye, wondering if he could stand to hear her admit her attraction to a man who did, but didn't exist. "What?"

"Never mind. Damn you, do you know what I went through?"

Anger spawned by hurt and pride flared suddenly and too fiercely to repress. "Did you pray for unconsciousness and even death because your doctor ran out of morphine before he could do any real repair work on you and the pain... holy mother, the pain was driving you mad? Did you step outside into the sun for the first time in—you weren't sure how long—only to have children run screaming at the sight of you?"

"Jon—"

"*Gabriel*. My...name...is...Gabriel," he growled, which made her raise a hand to her throat. "You can listen or you can tell me to go, but *don't* ask me if I ever wondered what my disappearance had done to you, because no matter what you might think, *that* was my real hell.''

Lisa shifted her hand to cover her face and she wept quietly. Wishing with every ounce of his being that she would let him go to her and hold her, he forced himself to retreat to the kitchen where he grabbed several tissues from the box he'd noticed before. Returning to the living room, he pressed them into her hand.

"I'm sorry," she sobbed.

"There's nothing to be ashamed of."

"No, I meant I was sorry for sounding like a selfish brat. Here I was lashing out against you for what I'd been through, but..." She mopped her eyes and wiped her nose. "I wasn't ignoring what you'd experienced, Jon, I mean G-Gabriel... Oh, damn, I'll never..." She fought for control and finally took a calming breath. "No matter how I feel about the rest, there aren't words to tell you how sorry I am for what you suffered."

"I don't want your pity."

"It's not pity."

"No? Well, forgive my bluntness, but you're not exactly throwing yourself into my arms out of passion, either!"

He watched her avert her face and barely held back the vicious curse that rose bitterly to his lips. To protect her from that, he spun away and rubbed his hands against his whisker-rough jaw. Three years of Oscar's sermons and philosophizing had sent him off with a hopeful heart that he'd grown to become a better man, but in a matter of hours he'd managed to forget everything he'd learned from the old savant.

"We can't go back to what we were," Lisa said sadly. "Too much has happened."

"I know." He sighed. "Forget I said that."

Lisa came up beside him. Slowly, tentatively, she lifted her hand to his left cheek. "This isn't as bad as you think."

"I've had operations," he replied tensely, aware his body was reacting to her touch, her warmth, as uncontrollably as a boy's. "Others, beyond those performed to save my life."

He could see that his reply confused her and removing her hand, she shook her head. "The same doctor you'd mentioned before?"

"No. Time and contingencies reduced Oscar's medical skills to that of removing shrapnel and mending broken bones. This was a friend of his who lived down—several hours away. He was a surgeon, who donated what medical supplies there were at the clinic."

"You started to say down...so you *were* up in the mountains, as you said last night?" She peered at him from beneath the sweep of her dark lashes. "How much of that story was true?"

"All of it," he replied, adding gruffly, "except that it wasn't me who was in the car when it exploded."

"Was it...the real Gabriel Ballesteros?"

"Until I created him, he didn't exist. No, the man who was killed was a contact I'd used on numerous trips to the country."

"I'm sorry. Was he a friend?"

"Work like ours isn't conducive to building friendships, but he was a good man."

"Did he have a family?"

"No."

"Perhaps that was best."

They stared at one another for several long seconds, his gaze asking if that was what she would have preferred and seeing the same question in hers. Grief mingled with memories and he came to no conclusions.

It was Lisa who broke the connection and retreated to the ficus tree by the windows. "I know you probably can't or won't tell me about your assignment, but... were you able to complete it?"

"I'm surprised you didn't charm that information out of Sennett, as well," Gabriel replied, beginning to scowl as he remembered what she'd gleaned so far.

His response only succeeded in earning him an arch look from Lisa. "Did you ever get to meet Sabra Sennett?"

He briefly recalled the wedding he'd almost missed and the redhead who'd so beguiled her husband-to-be that Sennett never noticed his best man was almost late with the ring. "We've met."

"Then you know how ridiculous that comment was. I couldn't 'charm' Mason if I'd put Sabra on a rocket to Mars and plied him with sour-mash whiskey to make him forget her," Lisa declared severely. "And I resent your suggesting that I'd stoop to that level."

"Don't underestimate your power," he said calmly. "You knocked me to my knees, didn't you?"

For an instant her defenses were lowered and he saw how much she wanted to believe that what they'd had was real, but just as quickly her caution returned. She plucked a yellowing leaf from the potted ficus. "What about your assignment? Were you successful?"

"Partly," he hedged. Then he reconsidered. *What the hell,* he told himself, *she'd earned the right to know.* Still, he couldn't help wonder if she was strong enough to handle such brutal honesty. "My assignment was to get the inside information on a rumored weapons deal being planned by an Argentinean armament supplier.

They sell routinely to Third World countries; however, because of changing world conditions their shrinking market share was making heretofore resisted deals more attractive. When certain countries came into the picture, our government wasn't thrilled with the idea that one of their South American allies might become a bedmate, if you will, to countries who'd labeled us forsworn enemies."

"What went wrong?"

"I inadvertently uncovered something just as problematic as our Middle Eastern troublemakers. The armament dealer wasn't the patriotic Argentinean he presented himself to be. He'd been using one of his private estates to build a military cache for a private army that he intended to use to overthrow his own government. But before we could get the information to Buenos Aires..." Gabriel's shrug was fatalistic.

Belatedly Lisa noticed her shaking fingers were rustling the leaves on the tree, and she withdrew them. "How did you ever survive?"

"Some villagers carried me to St. Jude's, the small mission run by Oscar O'Hearn."

"An Irishman in Argentina?"

"The U.S. isn't the only country that's a cultural melting pot. And Oscar's an Irish-American expatriate, to be exact. He was a doctor in one of those ancient overcrowded New York hospitals until he became one of the system's victims of burnout. Faced with a lawsuit that would probably strip him of his ability to continue in his profession, he became a vagabond, wandering the world. Somewhere along the way, he found religion and ended up starting St. Jude's mission."

"You mean he became something like a priest?"

"No, something like a zealot. Part physician, part priest, part naturalist, and all cartoonishly encased in a bean-pole body topped by orange hair that looks like a wig stolen from a Buenos Aires prostitute."

"He sounds...unique," Lisa murmured, allowing a hint of a smile.

It transformed her face, and in response, Gabriel's heart wrenched painfully. He risked his own brief smile and inclined his head. "The understatement of the century. Needless to say, ours was not a mutual-admiration society—at least not at the beginning."

"Still, he saved your life."

"Yes, my life. And Dr. Escobar made it possible for me to walk the streets like a human being again. But you," Gabriel said, his voice thickening with emotion, "you were what saved my sanity."

Lisa's eyes lit with hope and joy, but she quickly lowered her gaze to hide her thoughts and feelings from him. "What, um, happened to the arms dealer and his cache? Was he convinced you were dead?"

It took all of Gabriel's willpower not to kick over the end table in his anger. He couldn't believe she'd just listened to that confession and yet remained so...so unmoved. Had she changed that much?

If she has, you have only yourself to blame.

He raked his hand through his hair and, turning away, began to pace toward the opposite end of the room. "Not at first. His people weren't sure how many of us there had been. Oscar and his villagers took great risks hiding me from the men who came several times to comb the area. Later when I could, I figured out a way for the right people in the Argentinean government to find out what the dealer was up to, and he was forced to flee the country to save his own life."

"You mean he's out there somewhere free and capable of still hunting for you?" Lisa cried, aghast.

"Possibly, but I doubt it. At any rate, he would have to stand in line. There are others who would have more motive. No, he has bigger worries than me these days."

"You sound more . . . amused than relieved."

"The need for caution was a fact of life in my work," he admitted. "And I won't deny there was satisfaction in outwitting him. But, yes, I'm glad it appears to be over."

"And now?"

"I don't know."

Lisa's lips tensed, and Gabriel could almost feel her dissatisfaction and frustration with his answer. Good, he thought. He wasn't exactly feeling solid ground beneath his feet, either.

"I'd have thought you would at least have let Mason Sennett know you were alive," she told him.

"It crossed my mind. But my months of recuperation gave me a great deal of time to think. I came to the conclusion that this was the least-complicated way to handle things."

"Is that how you rationalized getting out of a marriage of convenience, too?"

He froze. It cost him a reserve of energy he didn't have, but he fought to restrain his temper again. "I never considered our marriage a mistake, and it damned well was never *convenient*."

"Really? Well, maybe you're right," Lisa said, twisting the clump of tissue in her hands. "Maybe it was more advantageous to have a wife back in the States mourning your death." She tried for a blithe laugh and only succeeded in a sob. "You should be proud of me. I really put on an award-winning performance."

It was too much. Gabriel crossed the room and, as she tried to run away from him, grabbed her shoulders and drew her back against his chest. "Don't," he rasped. "Don't do this to us. Haven't we been through enough?"

"Don't you know that I wanted to die, too?" she cried, as if he hadn't spoken. "When they told me, I wanted to stop breathing. It hurt too much even to do that."

"Ah, Lisa, do you think it was different for me?" he whispered against her hair. "At night when there was only darkness, I lay on my cot and dreamed you were with me, making love with me. And your hair—" he dared to touch it now "—this silk would follow your lips, soothing my feverish skin. I prayed never to wake up."

"I would cry myself to sleep because our bed was so empty."

"Sometimes when the wind blew gently, I pretended it was you singing carols on our first, our only, Christmas together. Dear God, I missed you."

"But not enough," she murmured sadly.

"That's not true! Damn it, this was to be my last assignment. I knew I couldn't keep leaving you like that. I wanted out."

"Then why?" she demanded, wrenching away and spinning around. "Why didn't you come back sooner?"

He drew himself erect, though his instincts told him to recede into the shadows, as had once been his professional preference. Now he only craved their emotional protection. "Things had changed. I decided you would be better off without me."

"*You* decided. You had no right to make that choice alone!"

With a groan that sounded more like a cry, Gabriel leaned toward her. "Look at this," he ground out, gesturing to his face. "This is as good as it's going to get! I had to come to terms with it myself."

Silence pulsated between them. He could see Lisa was upset over what she'd said, even ashamed. He didn't want that, and he couldn't bear it if she reached for him out of pity, so he withdrew and walked back toward the desk.

"We've become strangers, haven't we?" he asked at last.

"We always were strangers," she corrected wearily.

He picked up their wedding photo from her desk. "We loved."

"We made love."

He leaned back his head and laughed bitterly. "Ah, the precision of the teacher. All right then, we *made* love—but well. That should have counted for something."

"Passion has never been a wise basis for marriage. It doesn't last."

"No? Then why is this still on your desk?" he demanded, testing the frame's durability as he slammed the picture back on the tabletop. "Why are you still wearing my ring and that necklace? And why did you kiss me back in there?" he rasped, pointing toward the kitchen.

"I didn't know it was you until you said what you did about my eyes!"

That was one detail he wanted to ignore and he wheeled around, whether to curse her or wring her beautiful neck, he wasn't sure. But when he saw her ghostly pale face and tear-flooded eyes, the fight drained out of him and he knew he would rather lose his other eye than hurt her any further.

"You may try to convince yourself of that," he said, with what dignity he had left. "But in your heart of hearts you knew, Lisa. You *knew*." He had to believe that or go insane.

As they faced off, a clock in the back room chimed. It seemed to trigger something in Lisa and she closed her eyes. In the same spirit, Gabriel, feeling the past twelve hours taking its toll on his body, swayed on his feet.

"I'd better go," he said, wanting to leave before she noticed his condition. He glanced around, disoriented, trying to remember where he'd left his jacket. He needed to find someplace quiet and dark where he could rest. Think. Forget.

"Go where?" Lisa asked, following as he headed for the front door.

He could only tell her the truth. "I don't know. But I do know we've put each other through enough."

"Wait!"

He paused. Then, hesitantly, even reluctantly, he turned around, wondering if she had any idea what prolonging this was doing to him.

"You can't just go," she told him, edging closer. "Not like this. Besides, you . . . you're in no condition to travel."

"I can't stay here, either."

"Why not?"

The look he gave her spoke fathoms and had her cheeks turning a deeper shade of pink than they already were. "That's why," he said succinctly.

"We'll . . . we'll just have to work something out."

He arched his right eyebrow. "Don't forget your reputation. What will your friends say when they discover you have a stranger sleeping under your roof?"

"You're not a—"

Gabriel silenced her by gently touching his fingers to her lips. "You've already forgotten what I told you, *querida*. Jon Howard no longer exists."

He could feel her tremble, see the way her pupils dilated as she succumbed to his intimate touch. He wanted to revel in the knowledge that he could still affect her on this level, but he also knew it wouldn't be enough. He hadn't risked his life for a tempestuous kiss or even one night of passion with her, no matter how much he craved it. He wanted it all—a normal life...his wife...her love. Everything. Or he would settle for nothing.

"Then, um, take the cottage I offered you before I knew who— That I told you about," she said, glancing away in embarrassment. "I can have it cleaned up for you by this afternoon and I'll find some kind of draperies to cover the windows."

"Why?" he asked with the same intensity she'd had before.

"I'm not prepared to answer that right now."

He shook his head. "That's not good enough."

"Look," she groaned, rubbing her forehead, "all I know is that if I let you leave here now, I'll only end up feeling guilty and going out to look for you. You'll have to settle for that."

It was hardly what he'd dreamed when he'd imagined this moment. Then again, it wasn't the worst scenario he'd conjured in his mind. His Lisa had become a stronger woman; life, *he,* hadn't given her much choice. Oddly enough, it made her even more provocative. Did he really need the temptation?

Do you think you can take one step out that door and still call yourself alive?

"All right, I'll stay. For now. After all," he added, unable to hide all his bitterness, "who could refuse such an irresistable invitation?"

Five

"**Y**ou still don't look like you should be here."

Lisa glanced up from her as yet untouched soup and sandwich to see that Marie Thomas had arrived at the table they usually shared in the teachers' lounge. Hating to be a participant in any form of deception, but knowing she had to keep Jon's secret, Lisa summoned a reassuring smile for her friend and colleague. "It's Monday. I know you're always energetic and ready to go the minute your feet hit the floor in the morning, but most of us need a few hours to get our bearings. So how was Knoxville?" she added, eager to direct the subject away from herself.

"Fabulous." Marie set down her own lunch tray and slid into the seat across from Lisa. The fluid movement had her short blunt hairdo swinging, exposing gold hoop earrings that complemented the red highlights in her brown hair and her twinkling hazel eyes. "I found a bathing suit that's to die for. Leopard spots with a gold belt. Cut down to there and up to here...."

Nodding with amusement at Marie's dramatic pantomiming, Lisa scooped the slice of lemon out of her iced tea and laid it on the side of her plate. "You're going to be the belle of the cruise."

"Or go broke trying, right? Oh, Lisa, I wish you'd have let me talk you into going with us."

"With all the activities listed on that brochure you showed me, you, Linda and Ginny won't have time to miss me."

"But we've been like four musketeers since you came to Bentonville, and with Linda getting married in the fall, I wanted us four single girls to have a chance to experience one great vacation together."

Touched by her friend's affection and feeling slightly guilty about having to let the comment about "single girls" pass, Lisa kept her gaze lowered and offered an apologetic shrug. "I know, and I am sorry. But you also know how I feel about getting the house and those cottages done."

Marie grimaced and spread her napkin over her lap. "Don't remind me. That place has become such an obsession with you, I almost regret telling you about it. I don't know why you couldn't have settled for the house down the street from ours and lived in town like a normal person."

"There's nothing *ab*normal about liking the serenity of the woods. Besides, after living so close to a big city like Washington, D.C., I needed the space."

"Sure you did. All a person has to do is look at you and they can really see the improvement."

Frowning, Lisa glanced down at her pink suit with its white embroidered camisole discreetly exposed at the V neckline. She thought the outfit was professional yet feminine, an impression that was reinforced when Jon—*Gabriel*—had walked into the house to get a cup of coffee this morning and stopped dead in his tracks to stare at her.

"Is something wrong with my suit?" she asked, forcing herself to focus on Marie and her comment.

"Not the suit, *you*. From the looks of those shadows under your eyes, that bug you came down with Friday must have kept you awake all weekend. You're also stirring that soup as though you're still not convinced you can hold anything down. And you keep getting this dazed expression, so I know your mind hasn't returned from its excursion to Pluto."

It hadn't wandered that far, Lisa thought, shooting her friend a look of chagrin. But Marie was right. Her mind wasn't where it should be; it was still at home. She couldn't help but wonder what was going on there. What was he doing? Was he all right? Was he half as preoccupied with thoughts about her as she was about him?

They'd spent most of the weekend circling each other like wary strangers, searching for safe things to talk about, because after his explanation on Friday morning, both needed a break from the intensity of emotions churning between them. As a result, they'd been cautious with their questions, reluctant to probe into any sensitive areas.

Saturday had been slightly better because he'd spent most of the day sleeping, probably recovering from Friday's long dialogue, as well as the malaria attack. Lisa's stomach rolled threateningly as she remembered his story about the plane crash that she'd learned had been true. Ever since, her imagination had been working overtime and she'd wondered about the other horrors he'd experienced because of his line of work.

"See? There you go again!"

When Marie tapped the salt and pepper shakers together like cymbals, Lisa gave a startled jerk, followed by a grimace. "Sorry. I was thinking about something that happened this weekend," she said, realizing that her news had to come out sooner or later. There was no sense in delaying the inevitable.

"Let me guess. You reshingled all four cottages yourself?" Marie drawled sardonically. "No? Hmm. It couldn't be that you started tearing up those old porches, because you still have halfway decent-looking fingernails."

Shooting her a droll look, Lisa replied, "Have you by chance been testing your third-period class in world geography again? That always seems to do strange things to your sense of humor."

Marie nearly choked on a bite of her salad and hid her chuckle with her napkin. "You're getting to know me too well. Yes, indeed, if you ever want to hear answers that will bring tears to your eyes, come listen to Weldon Harley recite that Paraguay is part of Indonesia and that Sicily is the capital of Italy. Did I tell you that his current dilemma is finding Japan on my desk globe? I'm beginning to have this recurring nightmare where I'm this old thing, *still* teaching Weldon, not to mention half a dozen little Harleys." She rolled her eyes. "Don't let me get started. What was it that happened this weekend?"

After giving her friend a sympathetic look, Lisa forced herself to take a moment to taste a bit of chicken noodle soup; the way her heart was already pounding, she was afraid Marie would notice her unease before she even started her story. "I hired someone to help with the renovation work."

"Well, hallelujah and raise the flag. Who is it? The man I was telling you about that my parents used?"

"Um, no. I really was considering him," Lisa assured her, "but then, well, Gabriel came along and—"

"Gabriel? I don't think I know anyone around here named Gabriel."

"That's because he's not from here. He and Jon were…acquaintances. He was passing through the area and decided to look me up," Lisa said quickly, upon seeing her friend's surprise. Hoping she sounded convincing, she recited the story she and her husband had fabricated. "He's emigrating from Argentina and he's having some difficulty getting acclimated."

Marie rolled her eyes again. "So naturally that meant you had to take the old song about giving us your tired and your poor to heart and adopt him yourself? I swear, Lisa, you are the softest touch I've ever met. At least reassure me that you didn't put him up in your guest room. It's bad enough that you're living up there in the woods all by your lonesome, but with a stranger—"

"He's not in the guest room."

"At least that's something."

"He's in the first cottage."

Shaking her head, Marie jabbed her fork into her meat loaf. "I'm not going to tell Daddy about this. He thinks you're the sweetest thing since honeydew and it would upset him to no end if he heard how negligent you're being."

"Marie, he was Jon's friend."

"You said 'acquaintance' and you're usually meticulous in your choice of words."

Was everyone going to take potshots at her for that? "They knew each other well, all right? How could I not offer him some help? And if you'll think back, you were the one fussing at me the most to get someone to do the heavier work around the place."

"I suppose." Marie chewed thoughtfully. "What's he like?"

"He's . . . different."

"Different good, or different bad?"

"Just different."

"I'll bet he has a sexy voice." Marie's expression grew dreamy. "Latin men have the most luscious accents."

"Yes, well . . . he speaks excellent English."

"Married?"

Lisa glanced down at her wedding ring. "No."

"Good-looking?" Marie continued, her hazel eyes taking on a decided sparkle of interest.

The question was like a punch to Lisa's heart. "He was, I mean, he is, but not in a conventional way. He was in a car accident," she recited dutifully, though reluctantly. "He lost an eye and there's still some scarring on the left side of his face. He's very sensitive about it."

"Poor man," Marie murmured, considerably sobered. "I would imagine so." She remained thoughtful for a moment. "How long do you think he'll stay?"

Now there was a question Lisa hadn't contemplated, but one she wanted an answer to herself. "I don't know." With no small relief she spotted their friends. "Anyway, here come Ginny and Linda. Now you can tell me more about your shopping trip."

Lisa felt strange driving home that afternoon. With each passing mile, she was aware of every muscle in her body growing more tense and along with them her nerves, stretching to a point where her emotions were an indistinguishable mixture of anxiety and excitement. It wasn't unlike what she'd experienced the morning after her wedding night when she'd awakened cradled in the curve of her new husband's body. Then, too, she'd known an odd fright, yet an equally powerful euphoria, profoundly aware of the changes in her life.

And like that morning, she still couldn't believe this was real. Just like a phoenix rising from ashes, he'd returned. What did he want from her? What did she want from him? Would they ever get past the hurts and lies to a point where they could build anew?

The questions piled like lead weights in her mind, and by the time she was driving up the mountain, she had the beginnings of a tension headache throbbing at her temples and at the base of her neck. But as she turned into her dirt drive, thoughts of aspirin and a short nap gave way to surprise.

There he was balancing on a stepladder and cleaning out the front gutters on the house. The task was one she'd seen husbands do countless times as she drove around town, a task she'd been putting off for too long. But there was something so out of sync about his doing a chore that domestic, all she could do was stare.

Thinking he must have moved his own vehicle back near his cottage, she pulled her small sedan near the front steps and shut off the engine. Pilot, who'd been racing back and forth barking at the debris that fell from the gutters, rushed over to jump against the door. A sharp rebuke from Jon—try as she had thus far, it was still difficult to think of him as anything but Jon— had him docilely sitting down. Feeling more like a guest than the resident, Lisa got out of the car.

"I thought you'd never get home."

His words were innocent enough, yet the gruff tenderness in his voice gave them more meaning, which Lisa wasn't prepared to deal with yet. "Pushing your luck, aren't you?" she said instead, already feeling at a disadvantage since she had to look into the sun, while he had it at his back. She could almost feel his gaze moving over her and she belatedly wished she'd left on her jacket. The camisole, while cool and comfortable, left her feeling far too exposed.

"In what way?"

His voice was barely more than a murmur, which a slight breeze carried to her with a caressing stroke she felt over every inch of her body. "You... you were supposed to be taking it easy for the next few days, not try to discover how many lives you have left."

"The job needed to be done. Besides, keeping busy made the day pass more quickly."

The innuendo caused a tingling sensation to race over her bare arms. Wishing she could blame it on the sinking sun, she briskly rubbed herself and watched him descend the ladder.

It had been only a few days and already he looked stronger. His long lean muscles stretched and shifted under his jeans and T-shirt and his bronzed skin had a healthier luster from his having spent several hours in the fresh air.

"How was your day?" he asked huskily, when he stopped before her.

"Fine." Would he try to greet her with a kiss? she wondered. No, of course not; that wouldn't be wise to do in public. On the other hand, there was no public.

"You look pale."

Lisa gave herself a mental shake. "I'm always pale, remember?"

It was a mistake to ask. His gaze dropped to her breasts and Lisa knew he was remembering his fascination with the contrast between his dark hands and her fair body. She nearly groaned when she felt her nipples tighten in aching response.

"I remember." His T-shirt stretched with the deep breath he took. "And despite what you might tell me, I think your day was still a stressful one. I can see it here." He brushed the back of a finger against the corner of her compressed lips and repeated the caress at the outer corner of her eye. "And here."

His accent still rattled her, even as it intrigued. It was so elegant and charismatic, but it also reinforced her caution, reminding her of what a good actor he was. "We both knew it would be," she replied, struggling to keep her voice casual. "By the way, I announced that I'd hired a handyman. It went more smoothly than I'd anticipated."

"Deception always works best when one stays close to the truth."

"If you say so." Seeing that her words stung, she felt immediately contrite and added with more than a little awkwardness, "At least you can feel comfortable if you want to go into town for something. News has a way of making the rounds fast around here, so you needn't worry about people looking at you as if you were a complete stranger."

"It doesn't matter. I have no pressing desire to go down there."

She couldn't deny the surge of euphoria that gave her, but cautioned herself against being too gullible. She decided to shift to a safer subject. "Did you eat lunch?"

"Yes." His face relaxed into a tender smile. "Thank you for preparing the sandwich for me."

She'd left the house unlocked and had invited him to help himself to whatever was in the refrigerator, but she'd made a double-decker ham-and-cheese sandwich just in case he was hesitant about going to the trouble himself. She'd tried to convince herself that she would have done the same thing for anyone, but would anyone else's gratitude bring her such poignant pleasure?

"You're welcome. I'll start dinner as soon as—" Realizing what she'd begun to say, she silently berated herself, not only for the impulsive instigation of routines between them, but for assuming he would have dinner with her. After all, she'd already made it clear he should feel free to cook for himself in his own cabin; she'd even brought over a cardboard box of staples just in case. "I mean, would you like to join me?"

"Do you really think it necessary to ask?"

She dragged her gaze from his and struggled to come up with a safe reply. Instead she gestured at the gutters. "Thank you for that. I've been meaning to get to it, but something always seems to take precedence."

"To be perfectly honest, my motivation was based on pure selfishness. I started doing the one in back after deciding the next time it rained I didn't want to have to be half-drowned in order to get to you. And once I got started . . ."

The image of that first night, when he had walked through the waterfall on her front porch, flashed before Lisa's eyes, only this time her imagination got involved and she saw him take her in his arms, crush her close to his wet body and kiss her until his fever became hers. The thought made her blood race like a tempest and intensified the throbbing at her pulse points.

She massaged her temple where the throb was almost a pain. "Flirting with me isn't going to make this any easier."

"I wasn't flirting, Lisa. I was stating a simple fact." Stepping behind her, he brushed away her hand and replaced it with his own. "Is it bad?"

"It's getting there," she replied dryly.

"No thanks to me, eh?" He sighed. "I know you don't believe me, but I'm not pushing. However, neither do I intend to keep my feelings and thoughts to myself. You either want honesty or you don't, *querida*. You can't have it both ways."

Lisa closed her eyes and for a moment gave in to the need for his touch. "You're right...and I am trying."

"I can see that."

His fingers, strong yet gentle, felt wonderful, and with the sun bathing her face, she was soon enfolded in a warm cocoon of peace. But when she felt his lips brush the hair near her ear, caution came back in a panicky skid.

"I'd better go inside and change," she murmured, carefully drawing away from him. Though she turned to face him, she hugged her purse, jacket and books like a shield to her chest. "I'll get started on dinner in a few minutes."

"There's no rush. I can wait."

"Well, then maybe I'll take a shower first."

"And perhaps lie down for a few minutes." He gave her a secret smile. "I don't think you've outgrown a child's need for afternoon naps."

The seductive warmth pervading her body intensified as she recalled how, in the short time they'd had together, he'd also come to enjoy those naps. *Too fast,* her inner voice warned and she firmly shook her head. "I told you, I've changed."

If he was unconvinced or disappointed he hid it well, and after another moment, when it became clear he had nothing else to say, she excused herself and hurried into the house. What she didn't escape was the knowledge that she'd behaved with a coldheartedness she'd never believed herself capable of.

She was afraid. He felt her fear and even under-stood, but that didn't make finding the patience to deal with it any easier. As Gabriel leaned back in the dinette chair and watched Lisa rinse the last of the dinner dishes, he wondered what he could do to make things easier on them both.

Leave.

He dismissed the thought as soon as it came to him. Leaving was no longer an option. It may have been back at the mission when Oscar played devil's advocate and reminded him of all the things that could go wrong, along with the reasons Lisa would be better off think-ing he was dead. But not now.

At the same time, he didn't know how much more he could stand of this wall of formal politeness she was hiding behind, either. If all he'd had was a proclivity for excellent food and safe conversation, he could have dialed Sennett's number and been in a Washington high-rise hotel eating food from room service, sipping on expensive Scotch and having the television talk to him.

He wanted more.

Wouldn't Oscar be shaking his head if he could hear this? And be full of advice? "The eagle has no business envying the canary that has been born and raised in captivity," he would say again. "Freedom and domesticity are natural opposites, and trying to convince her that you could achieve a happy medium between the two will only bring you frustration and her a wariness of the contradiction in you."

Yet that was what he was—a walking contradiction or, rather, what he'd become when he'd taken on his new name and strived to make a different life for himself. He didn't blame Lisa for being skittish; it had taken him time to get used to the evolution of changes in himself, as well. He respected her caution and need to get a better understanding of the man she'd married. The problem was that that man no longer existed, at least not in his original form. Gabriel had survived what Jon hadn't been able to. As a result, the changes went far beyond the physical. And they were for the better, he truly believed that. But getting Lisa to give him the chance to prove it to her was becoming the ultimate challenge.

"Why don't you leave that and come out for a walk with me while it's still light?" he suggested, pushing himself to his feet. He had to move. Just sitting there watching her in that casual red velour jumpsuit was taking its toll on his imagination. One of those spaghetti-thin straps kept slipping off her shoulder and he was tempted to go help it along. He wanted to slide both straps down her arms, the bodice, too, then strip out of his T-shirt and—

"I should go over my lessons for tomorrow," she said, breaking into his fantasies.

With a shake of his head, he crossed over to her and took the towel out of her hands. He set it on the counter, then linked his fingers with hers. "I have a feeling tomorrow's lessons are pure rote to you by now, and the next day's, as well. Come out with me and show me this land of yours."

"I would have thought you'd already made a thorough tour of the place."

"I wanted to wait for you. See it from your perspective."

He liked the heightened color his words brought to her face and, drawing her with him, escorted her outside. Pilot, never far from the house, came happily to join them, dropping the ball in his mouth, clearly eager to abandon it for the more satisfying chance to go exploring.

"How long have you had him?" Gabriel asked, releasing her to find and throw a stick for the dog.

"Two and a half years. Sometimes I think he saved my life."

He shot her a sharp look. "In what way?"

"He made me stop thinking about myself. Gave me a purpose that work alone couldn't."

Gabriel brooded over that. If he had left her with a baby, maybe she wouldn't have felt so alone and useless. Yet even as he thought that, he knew they hadn't been ready for children; certainly he hadn't been ready. Amazed and, yes, dubious of fate's gift of letting him find her at all, he'd allowed himself to be selfish, wanting Lisa to be completely his for a while. Back then he hadn't believed anything so good could be real, let alone last.

They walked past his cottage on the right and the next on the left, both aged cedar buildings that were as rustic on the inside as they appeared on the outside. Then they stepped onto a rickety footbridge that straddled a brisk-flowing brook. Midway, Lisa paused to watch the water, clean and clear and sunlit in spots, shimmering with amber and silver lights in others, as it skipped over and around stones and fallen tree limbs.

"This is what sold me," she said, smiling as she listened to the mystically melodic sounds.

"You always were drawn to water. That's why I was somewhat taken by surprise when I learned you'd moved away from our home. I knew you'd loved being close to Chesapeake Bay." On one of their first dates they'd rented a sailboat. The next time out, he'd borrowed Sennett's cabin cruiser, and it was there they'd first made love.

"Were you disappointed to find I'd left?"

"Would it matter to you if I was?"

She turned to face him fully. "I'd like to know, yes."

Lord, but she was lovely like this, he thought, taking in her hair, lifted gently by the breeze. The setting sun warmed each silken strand to a honey color. And the way her gentle eyes studied him so somberly made him feel acutely the pain of loving her. "No," he replied softly. "It wouldn't have mattered if you'd decided to move to an igloo in the North Pole. I would have looked for you."

Her chuckle was forced and she shifted her gaze back to the brook. "You couldn't have been too worried about having to search too far. You already knew I'm not overly fond of endlessly long winters."

Memories washed over him like mulled wine. "Yes. You used to tell me your toes and fingers become like icicles by autumn's first frost—always before using me to defrost them." And he also remembered that no matter what time of the day or night it occurred, they would inevitably end up making love.

You may be the winner of the

MILLION DOLLAR
GRAND PRIZE!

$1,000,000.00	**MILLION**	$1,000,000.00
	DOLLAR GRAND PRIZE	
	SWEEPSTAKES ENTRY STICKER	
$1,000,000.00		$1,000,000.00

OVER EIGHT THOUSAND OTHER PRIZES	WIN A MUSTANG BONUS PRIZE	WIN THE ALOHA HAWAII VACATION BONUS PRIZE
Guaranteed FOUR FREE BOOKS No obligation to buy!	Guaranteed FREE VICTORIAN PICTURE FRAME No cost!	Guaranteed PLUS A MYSTERY GIFT Absolutely free!

ENTER SILHOUETTE'S BIGGEST SWEEPSTAKES EVER!

IT'S FUN! IT'S FREE!
AND YOU COULD BE A
MILLIONAIRE!

Your unique Sweepstakes Entry Number appears on the Sweepstakes Entry Form. When you affix your Sweepstakes Entry Sticker to your Form, you're in the running, and could be the $1,000,000.00 annuity Grand Prize Winner! That's $33,333.33 every year for up to 30 years!

AFFIX BONUS PRIZE STICKER

to your Sweepstakes Entry Form. If you have a winning number, you could collect any of 8,617 prizes. And we'll also enter you in a special bonus drawing for a new Ford Mustang and the "Aloha Hawaii Vacation"!

AFFIX FREE BOOKS
AND GIFTS STICKER

to take advantage of our Free Books/Free Gifts introduction to the Silhouette Reader Service™. You'll get four brand-new Silhouette Desire® novels, plus a lovely Victorian picture frame and a mystery gift, absolutely free!

NO PURCHASE NECESSARY!

Accepting free books and gifts places you under no obligation to buy a thing! After receiving your free books, if you don't wish to receive any further volumes, write "cancel" on the shipping document and return it to us. But if you choose to remain with the Silhouette Reader Service, you'll receive six more Silhouette Desire novels every month for just $2.47* each—28¢ below the cover price, with no additional charge for delivery. You can cancel at any time by dropping us a line, or by returning a shipment to us at our cost. Even if you cancel, your first four books, your lovely Victorian picture frame and your mystery gift are absolutely free—our way of thanking you for giving the Reader Service a try!

*Terms and prices subject to change without notice. Sales tax applicable in NY.
© 1990 HARLEQUIN ENTERPRISES LIMITED

This lovely Victorian pewter-finish miniature is perfect for displaying a treasured photograph. And it's yours FREE as added thanks for giving our Reader Service a try!

Silhouette Reader Service™   Sweepstakes Entry Form

This is your **unique** Sweepstakes Entry Number: 2D 366714

> This could be your lucky day! If you have the winning number, you could be the Grand Prize Winner. To be eligible, *affix Sweepstakes Entry Sticker here!* **(SEE RULES IN BACK OF BOOK FOR DETAILS)**

> If you would like a chance to win the $25,000.00 prize, the $10,000.00 prize, or one of many $5,000.00, $1,000.00, $250.00 or $10.00 prizes ... plus the Mustang and the Hawaiian Vacation, *affix Bonus Prize Sticker here!*

> To receive free books and gifts with no obligation to buy, as explained on the **opposite page,** *affix the Free Books and Gifts Sticker here!*

Please enter me in the sweepstakes and, when the winner is drawn, tell me if I've won the $1,000,000.00 Grand Prize! Also tell me if I've won any other prize, including the car and the vacation prize. Please ship me the free books and gifts I've requested with sticker above. Entering the Sweepstakes costs me nothing and places me under no obligation to buy! (If you do not wish to receive free books and gifts, do not affix the FREE BOOKS and GIFTS sticker.)

225 CIS ACL2

YOUR NAME	PLEASE PRINT	
ADDRESS		APT#
CITY	STATE	ZIP

Silhouette "No Risk" Guarantee

- You're not required to buy a single book—ever!
- As a subscriber, you must be completely satisfied or you may cancel at any time by marking "cancel" on your statement or by returning a shipment of books at our cost.
- The free books and gifts you receive are yours to keep.

ALTERNATE MEANS OF ENTRY: Print your name and address on a 3" x 5" piece of plain paper and send to: Silhouette's Wishbook Sweepstakes, 3010 Walden Ave., P.O. Box 1867, Buffalo, N.Y. 14269-1867

"You complained I was using you to lower the heating bills."

He wasn't fooled by her dry-witted reply; he could see by the sudden shallowness of her breathing that she remembered the rest as vividly as he did. "A superfluous gesture made only because you expected it."

His suavely spoken response earned him an amused look, before Lisa withdrew and continued the rest of the way across the bridge. Stepping onto land again, she indicated where Pilot had gone to inspect an old tree with a big hole in its base. "I think it'll have to come down. It's too close to that third cabin. After several months of watching the way the wind can blow around here, I know it's just a matter of time before I get up one morning and find it sticking through the roof. And I certainly don't want that to happen when someone's renting the place."

She led him toward the right and along a meandering path that cut more deeply into the woods. They came to a soft spot where the runoff of water from Thursday's rain still stood and the ground remained muddy. Glancing down, she spotted the tracks that proved he and Pilot had already been exploring.

"So, you haven't seen the place yet," she drawled.

"It was Pilot's idea, not mine," he teased. Then he added more seriously, "You've become quite the observant one."

She shrugged away the compliment. "It's just that I keep an eye out for the four-legged variety of tracks. We're known to have black bear here, and while I haven't come face-to-face with one myself, I understand it's not an impossibility."

"There were two does grazing here this morning after you left."

"A pregnant one and the other slightly smaller?" When he nodded, Lisa smiled with satisfaction. "Mother and daughter. Getting Pilot to learn not to chase them has been a chore."

They walked until they came to a sturdy barbed-wire fence. "Who owns the land beyond this?" Gabriel asked.

"It's part of the national forest. I really like the idea of being adjacent to it. This way I don't have to worry about anyone coming in and clearing away the woods, as they might if it was privately owned. Isn't it wonderful?"

"Lisa," he began, focusing on something that had been in the forefront of his mind. "Financially, are you all right?" He knew a teacher's income might be enough to maintain this place, but not enough for renovation. He hated to think she was spending her entire inheritance from her parents to achieve it.

"I'm fine," she assured him, adding with a touch of humor, "I'm disgustingly frugal." Then she grew serious. "You must know that Mason made sure I received your pension since you were declared dead. I consulted with a financial expert and had it invested, but by rights it *is* yours."

"Don't be ridiculous."

"I'm serious."

"I have what I need," he muttered, though he wasn't about to go into how individuals in his line of work always kept cash accessible. "I only wanted to be certain you were cared for and content, and it's clear you are." He could see it in her face as she observed her surroundings. Was his presence enhancing that or detracting from it?

They came to a cutoff and she motioned to the path on the right, saying it led back to the house. After a moment she murmured, "Tell me about where you've been living."

He would have preferred listening to her, but he understood it was time to share something of himself. "The mission is in the northern part of the country, in the mountains, an area of dense vegetation. Farming is the basis of most people's incomes, and the majority of them are poor. Oscar built St. Jude's out of whatever scraps of material he could find, buy or steal. Some buildings are even made out of airplane wreckage."

He paused to watch a squirrel scurry up a tree, then continued. "There are about thirty permanent residents at the mission, though the total population fluctuates depending on what disease is running rampant through the villages, who's been forced from their homes by floods and the various other tragedies that seem to strike the poor more frequently than others. And there are the occasional orphans. Oscar works hardest at finding them homes."

"How do the residents survive?" Lisa asked him. "Is it a self-sufficient community?"

"They try to be. Women weave baskets to be taken down into the cities and sold. Some of the men had a talent for leather working and wood carving, so when the farming isn't bringing in what they need, they can make ends meet by turning to other marketable skills. Still, it's not an easy life."

"Yet you stayed longer than you needed to."

"A person can get used to anything, if he tries hard enough. Besides, I'd been trained for surviving in even worse conditions. It wasn't difficult in that respect. If I could have forgotten you, it would have been as good a place as any to spend the rest of my life."

They'd reached the bridge again and Lisa, stumbling over what must have been a raised nail, lost her balance. Gabriel grabbed her before she could fall.

Using his entire body to steady her, he felt his inevitable instant reaction, the awareness and arousal that was the price he paid for his sensitivity to her. But knowing it would be a mistake to force her to give him more than her momentary trust, he simply held her against him and lowered his head beside hers.

"Let me have this much," he whispered, feeling the slight tremor that raced through her. "You don't know what simply holding you does to me."

She didn't reply, but neither did she pull away. After a moment, he closed his eyes in contentment. "Thank you," he murmured.

"You make me feel ashamed for holding you at arm's length."

The sadness underlying her voice touched his heart. "Don't. I do understand your reasons."

Slowly she relaxed and laid her head against his shoulder. "I enjoyed our walk."

"Did you?"

"Mmm. It reminded me of the long walks we took on our honeymoon."

They'd wandered along miles of beach and sat in the surf until the sun set, often so content with each other that they didn't bother to speak.

"Then you don't regret everything we shared?"

"There have been times I wish I could, but no, I don't."

He closed his eyes again. "We were good together."

"I think I was a novelty to you. You liked the effect you had on me."

That made him raise his head to search her face for resentment, but he found none. "I think we liked the effect we had on each other," he replied, allowing himself the luxury of stroking her back. She felt so good, so right in his arms, he couldn't help but ask, "Can you say you've felt like this with anyone since?"

It wasn't really a fair question, and as he expected, her chin rose. "I could ask the same thing."

"In which case I would reply that I might as well have been a monk in that mission, because I never wanted another woman but you." He shifted his hold to frame her face with one hand. "Would I be a fool for hoping it was the same for you?"

"I thought I made that embarrassingly clear the other day."

His body responded to that, as well, and with a muffled groan, he drew her more firmly against the intensifying ache centering in his lower body. "You're my *wife*. How can you be embarrassed to tell me anything."

"Jon Howard doesn't exist anymore, remember?"

"Perhaps not to the rest of the world, but you know that no matter what happens between us, under at least one law, you'll always belong to me."

"What are you saying?" she whispered, pulling away. "Was that supposed to be some kind of a threat?"

"No, a fact. We made vows to each other before God, Lisa."

She shook her head. "Don't you dare throw that in my face. I'm not the one who took off the wedding band."

"I had no choice. Hell's fury, you know me better than that!"

"No, that's the problem. You keep saying things you think I want to hear, but the man beneath the smooth lines is still a stranger."

"Perhaps it's because I'm finding it disconcerting to discover that the woman I adored now puts restrictions on her feelings."

"That's not fair!"

"You want to discuss fairness? You can barely bring yourself to say my name."

"Because it's just another camouflage you're using to hide who you really are!" she cried.

Gabriel knew she was right and, releasing her, he spun away and slammed his hands against the wooden railing. What was wrong with him? For a few minutes everything had been going so well; the distance between them had actually seemed to shrink. Now, because he'd given in to impatience, the chasm was between them again.

He heard a buzzing near his face and he brushed at it. "Maybe it's time for you to go on inside," he told her, unable and unwilling to hide his growing desolation. "The mosquitoes are starting to come out."

The ancient boards creaked only faintly under Lisa's slight weight and then he felt her touch his shoulder. It cost him not to reach up and cover her hand with his.

"I didn't mean to hurt you," she murmured sadly.

"I wasn't exactly being kind myself."

He could feel her hesitate, debate. "Will you be all right?" she finally asked.

As all right as any man can be when his body is screaming to rediscover the pleasure and relief of mak-

ing love to his wife. "I have a talent for survival, remember?"

With a sigh, she stepped around him. He let her get back onto the path toward her house before he called after her. "Don't punish yourself over this, Lisa. Try to sleep peacefully."

She'd turned at the first sound of his voice, and when he was through, she gave him a faint sad smile. "You, too. Good night . . . Gabriel."

His heart in his throat, he watched her until she slipped into the house. "Good night, my love," he whispered hoarsely.

Six

Friday afternoon, as she climbed out of her car, the reverberating thunder of what sounded like a sledgehammer beating against the house made Lisa freeze in place. *What in the world...?*

In the silence that followed, she looked around trying to discern where the noise had come from, though she knew she was at a disadvantage. She was standing beneath an umbrella of trees, which gave sound a boxed-in quality, making it difficult to tell.

Soon, however, another series of rhythmic resonating blows began, this time accompanied by Pilot's barking. She still didn't have any idea what was going on, but from the enthusiastic—rather than ferocious—clamoring, she had to assume Gabriel was tackling yet another project and her pet was providing moral support.

With more curiosity than relief, she shut the car door and, carrying her purse and books, hurried along the walk to her house. She couldn't have found someone who was more hardworking if she had advertised in the local newspaper. He was proving to be relentless. But she understood what was driving him, what had been driving him all week, and it wasn't a great love for hard labor; it was frustration... tension... nerves.

She wasn't immune to them herself. In fact today alone there had been several instances when she'd found herself thinking of how good it would feel to throw or even hit something. Hard. Thank goodness she'd made it through the week without giving in to the temptation. She deplored violence; she'd never even been able to stand watching a boxing match on television. The very notion of two otherwise seemingly sane people trying to beat the other to a mindless pulp, even for money, was incomprehensible to her.

Well, just one more week, she reassured herself as she thrust her key into the door lock, and school would be out for the summer. Then she could stop pretending— at least to her students and colleagues—that everything was all right and she was fine.

Once inside she crossed to her desk and gratefully deposited her books, purse and the mail she'd picked up from her post-office box. Without a second look to check if the deluge stayed put or was about to spill to the floor, she dashed to the window. And there she saw him, literally and figuratively putting his back into breaking down the rotting front porch of his cottage.

Sometime during the past week, when she hadn't been at school and they were doing more than filling the long stretches of silence between them with hardly significant but safe conversation, she'd mentioned she planned to rip it out and have it replaced. She should have known he would give the project immediate priority, just as she didn't doubt he'd already put in a full day on something else.

Apparently, he'd decided he still had an ounce or two of energy left and didn't want to stop until he had totally exhausted himself. What better way to ensure that, when he finally did crawl into bed tonight, he would actually sleep instead of tossing and turning. She understood the motivation; she had been practicing a variation of it herself.

But there was such a thing as pushing oneself to the extreme. She wanted to make him ease up, especially when she knew she was to blame for his current state of mind. But what could she do? Since the incident on the bridge, things had only become shakier between them instead of better. Overnight he'd done some sort of reversal on her; he'd made it clear that if all she was offering him at this point was service as a cook or nursemaid, he could do without her company. Then from dawn to dusk he worked at anything and everything he could to preoccupy his mind. She recognized that tactic, too, because she was almost as bad. In a way, the situation between them had been reduced to a ridiculous unspoken contest; it was as if they were both out to see who was going to drop from exhaustion first.

"Oh, Gabriel," she whispered.

At least he had won *that* from her. Their relationship might not be making the progress he would like, but at least she was beginning to think of him the way he wanted; not as Jon, but as Gabriel—proud, egocentric, even tyrannical, though he was careful how he exhibited that trait. They were features she would never have thought to attribute to Jon and none she cared, or was willing, to yield to now.

That he wanted her back in his life and in his bed, she understood; she could even sympathize with the disappointment and frustration she was putting him through. After all, was it so different from her own? She still desired, she still loved, but she'd also come to learn there was more to making a marriage work than good sex and love. No, she couldn't give in, not until, not unless, she saw some hope they could resolve their problems.

The irony was that, like Jon, Lisa—at least the old Lisa—no longer existed, and she was having difficulty making him accept that. He couldn't or wouldn't believe she had completely outgrown the woman she'd been, yet she was supposed to accept Gabriel Ballesteros like a new improved brand of breakfast cereal because he believed her faith and uncontested devotion was still as accessible as her passion.

As a result, they had come to a stalemate. An emotional impasse—while the sexuality simmering between them intensified with every second, whether they were together or not.

How long were they going to be able to continue like this? she wondered. She had lost her ability for blind trust; he, on the other hand, wanted to step back to a special time that in reality had been as tenuous as vapor. Sometimes she wondered if they were foolish to think that there might be middle ground. What kind of future could they hope for when each of them bore so many scars and so many blind spots?

She blinked and refocused on the man working. Her husband. Yet not her husband. A stranger. Yet not a stranger. Her nails had once scored that tautly muscled back in passion. Now his bronzed flesh was glistening with the sweat of a different physical exertion. She had wrapped her legs around those lean hips in a sensual dance as old as time. Though his lower body was hidden from her by low-slung jeans and no doubt bore new scars, she knew her body would still fit his with a unique perfection that only emphasized nature's mysteries.

She saw him pause and wearily drag his forearm across his sweating brow. Chest heaving, he stared up at the sky. Lisa could almost feel his desolation, and beneath her breast, her heart ached with empathy.

Enough was enough. They both needed a break. Following an impulse she knew would be dangerous to overanalyze, she went into the kitchen and reached into the refrigerator for one of the beers she now kept on hand especially for him. Using a paper towel to twist off the screw cap, she went outside to take it to him. It was Friday, she told herself when, despite her attempts not to think about what she was doing, her subconscious began to chide her crumbling resolve. It was time for some kind of armistice.

As usual, it was Pilot who spotted her first. Gabriel had returned to his work, ripping nails out of the boards he'd already removed with the claw end of a hammer. The dog stood on the porch barking bravely at the tool. When he saw her, he leapt down and bounded toward her.

Trying to balance herself against his friendly assault, Lisa scratched the top of his head and held aloft the beer she carried in her other hand. When she was close enough, she offered it to Gabriel, who'd been watching her from the moment Pilot had bolted.

"You look like you could use this," she murmured, aware of the way her heart was pounding and how dry her own throat had suddenly become.

He considered the bottle for what seemed like an eternity and Lisa knew he was remembering how, in the first days of their relationship, once she'd learned his preference was for imported beer and that he liked it in bottles instead of cans, she'd never bought anything else.

"Thank you." He shifted his gaze to her, did a slow thorough inspection in that habitual way that made Lisa glad she looked her best today. She was wearing the lavender blouse and slim violet skirt she'd purchased only a few weeks before his arrival. Only when he was through did he lift the bottle to his lips and take a long drink. Afterward he made a deep-throated sound of satisfaction. "I needed that."

Lisa lifted an eyebrow at the half-empty bottle. "Maybe I should have brought two."

"Then I'd start feeling sluggish and never finish this," he replied, inclining his head toward the porch. "Aren't you home early?"

Actually, she was right on time with her normal schedule, but with the increased tension between them, lately she'd been lingering at school longer than usual. Not wanting to explain that, she shrugged and countered with a question of her own. "Why are you doing the hardest work during the hottest hours of the day?"

"It's dangerous to leave it this way. I almost fell through a rotten board earlier today and I decided I didn't want to take a chance of you wandering back here and hurting yourself."

The chance of her "wandering" anywhere near him was less than slight. She would either come intentionally, like now, or not at all. But she ignored that to concentrate on him. "Are you all right?" she asked, looking for any signs of injury.

He shook his head. "Quick reflexes saved me."

"You know, you're already working hard enough for two men, and considering that it wasn't too long ago that you were flat on your back, maybe—"

"I'm fine."

There was no missing the clipped quality of his voice, and understanding that he didn't want to be continually reminded of his previous weakness, she bit her lip. "Excuse me. Of course you know best."

Silence stretched and he took another drink. Lisa pretended an interest in the new weeds once again showing up in her flower beds and the rapidly growing grass. She grazed the tallest blades with her sandaled foot. "I know it's a good thing we're getting plenty of rain, but it does make everything around here sprout like a tropical rain forest, doesn't it? I'm glad school will be out soon so I'll have more time to keep up with things."

"I'll second that."

Lisa shot him a startled look, only to see the flicker of humor in his eye. Catching on, a soft throaty laugh bubbled from deep inside her. "Misery loves company, eh?"

"Something like that. Besides, your dog is a pain when you're not around. He either lies underfoot moping, or drives me crazy barking at every hammer, saw or rake I reach for."

She smiled down at her pet, who right now was the picture of obedience, calmly sitting at her feet and leaning the bulk of his weight against her leg. "How nice to be missed."

"Mmm . . . by him at least."

As Gabriel lifted the bottle and tilted back his head to swallow the rest of his beer, Lisa silently regretted her blunder. But what could she say that she hadn't already to make him understand she *was* trying to resolve her conflicting feelings toward him? Good heavens, didn't he remember she was the one who'd insisted he stay on? Didn't he recognize this was no easier on her than it was on him?

Before she could reply he was grimacing and rubbing the back of his neck. "Forget I said that—if you can."

"I know I haven't been the easiest person to get along with lately," she replied.

"Neither of us would win any awards. But then I don't suppose this is a contest."

"Then you do understand?"

"Yes, though it doesn't mean I have to like it."

Still, Lisa could find some comfort in that. "Fair enough."

A bumblebee, sounding like an overloaded military helicopter, descended on a nearby anemone, nearly bending it to the ground. Lisa's heart felt that heavy. Above, a faint breeze stirred the treetops. She ached for the relief it would bring, because the man beside her, who now seemed fascinated with the remnants of foam sliding down the inside neck of his bottle, made her feel as though she was suffering from a constant low-grade fever.

"Will you freeze on me again if I tell you that you look lovely in that color?" He didn't wait for her to reply, and the truth was she couldn't have thought of anything to say if she wanted to. "I came across a patch of columbine in those very shades this morning. I'll have to show it to you."

Lisa had once told him his gift for smooth talk could flatter a shark out of his dinner or convince a woman to toss her last tube of lipstick in the trash, and even now his compliment brought a rush of pleasure. But she knew it would be wiser not to let him see how much and to keep their mood as light as possible. "Have you taken to indulging in nature walks every morning?"

"I've always maintained the practice in isolated areas."

Whatever reply she'd expected, it wasn't that. Unless she was mistaken, what he was really doing was something like a perimeter search. The very concept was foreign to her, not to mention disturbing. "Surely you don't think . . . You said you thought all threats against you were over?"

"And I meant it. But it doesn't mean I'm going to abandon common sense—particularly when my neglect could hurt you. Besides," he continued, cutting off her protest, "I told you I was in Washington before I came here. And while I was careful, it doesn't alter the fact that if you thought you saw something familiar in me, someone there might have, as well."

"Have you seen any signs of anything suspicious?" she asked, glancing around. Until he'd spoken, the woods had always seemed so peaceful and unthreatening. Had she once again been guilty of naïveté?

"Nothing except the usual flora and fauna. Oh, and a particularly overburdened mother opossum taxiing her brood home after a night's feasting."

Lisa saw his tender reassuring smile and searched for a sign that it was a bluff. She found none and relaxed enough to wrinkle her nose. "As the girls in my class would say, 'Ugh.'"

"You don't like opossum?"

"They look like big rats."

"True, but weigh their presence against the options of having to share the area with rats, or better yet, as many skunks," he drawled.

"Ah, you have a point." She chuckled lightly. "On second thought, I suppose they're harmless enough."

She liked him this way, playful and with a complete absence of any emotional pressure that only casual talk allowed. If only they could prolong it.

"What are you thinking? You look almost—dare I say it—happy."

"We're not negotiating over lost ground," she replied, her tone dry. "And I was just remembering part of the reason I came out here. Do you think we could make the mood last long enough to have dinner tonight? I know you made it clear you were perfectly capable of getting your own meals," she said quickly upon seeing the veil of caution once again shadow his eye. "But, well, it is Friday, and dare I say it? I'm sick of my own company."

He seemed to consider the invitation forever, and when he leaned over and set the empty beer bottle on the edge of the porch, Lisa began to wonder if he would answer at all. "It depends," he finally told her.

That dampened her spirits somewhat and, prepared for the worst, she asked, "On what?"

"What are we having?" he asked, as somberly as if they had been discussing the effect of some current government policy on the stock market.

She folded her arms across her chest and with equal earnestness replied, "Pot luck. After all, I only just decided to make the offer."

"A definite gamble. All right—as long as it's nothing with tomatoes or beans, and *definitely* nothing with peppers. I've had enough of all three to last me a life-time.''

Lisa recalled his favorite meal used to be sweet-and-sour shrimp. She was certain she had some shrimp in her freezer, as well as the other necessary ingredients. When she suggested it to him, his response, the surprised touched expression that fleetingly exposed his vulnerable feelings, had her heart melting like an ice cube in a broiler.

''You remember,'' he said gruffly.

''Of course.''

''It's been a long time, and I don't recall having mentioned it.''

''But you ordered it at every Oriental restaurant we ever went to,'' she pointed out, softening her mockery with a smile.

He smiled, too. The air between them suddenly blossomed with an intoxicating sweetness, and Gabriel, murmuring her name, took a step toward her.

She knew she should take a step back, crack a joke, ask him about the kind of lumber he thought best to use for the porch. But her feet wouldn't move and her brain seemed to be stuck in neutral.

''Excuse me . . . Mrs. Howard? Mrs. Lisa Howard?''

She heard her name called twice and even saw Gabriel stiffening before she snapped out of her stupor and spun around to see who their untimely intruder was. Approaching from her patio was a blond-haired man in a conservative gray suit. Even to her inexperienced eye, she could see something about him that evoked authority.

She hadn't begun to acknowledge his question when Pilot, already barking, set off in an impressive charge. ''Pilot, heel!'' she called. Of course there was no reason for the dog to pay attention to her since she'd never used the directive before. Instead Pilot made a wide circle around the man and continued his tirade.

Lisa glanced back at Gabriel and whispered, "Does he look like someone in the government or am I just getting paranoid?"

"He's probably connected."

"Then I shouldn't let him get too close to you. I'll go invite him into the house," she said quickly.

"No!" The urgent reply was barely audible above Pilot's fierce bellowing. "Let's find out who he is and what he wants first."

"Are you crazy?"

"Are *you?* I'll wager the dinner you just offered me that he's wearing a gun under that tailored jacket. That's reason enough not to leave you alone with him."

Lisa didn't know what shocked her more, the idea that the man—who, upon closer inspection, looked more like a junior bank executive—could be concealing a weapon, or her sudden sense of leashed danger in Gabriel. But as he shifted a protective inch or two closer to her, she reminded herself that if their act was to be credible, there was a performance to put on.

She gave herself a mental shake and focused on what needed to be handled immediately. "Pilot," she called, her voice suddenly a half octave higher and wheedling. "Come here, sweetheart."

The dog shot her a mild look over his shoulder, as if he couldn't believe his ears, but at least he deigned to trot back to her side. The young man—Lisa could now determine he was probably no more than a few years older than she was—approached with caution.

"I'm sorry," she told him, hoping her smile didn't look as brittle as it felt. "I'm afraid he's extremely territorial."

"And big. Er, are you Mrs. Howard?"

"Yes, I am. What can I do for you?"

The man's gaze shifted to Gabriel a second before he reached into his jacket. His clean-cut, boy-next-door look truly did inspire confidence and openness, and had Gabriel not warned her, Lisa was sure she would easily have let down her guard. Now, however, she found herself tensing, until the hand reappeared with only a leather case. She could only imagine how Gabriel felt, but she didn't look at him.

The man flashed his badge and identification, and she had her first taste of how difficult it was to try to concentrate on reading those things when your adrenaline was flowing. In the space of seconds she decided all the actors on TV should be spritzed and should drink ten cups of black coffee before taping such scenes, because she could already feel a trickle of sweat slide down her back and she was shaking as though she'd overdosed on caffeine.

"The name's Talbert, ma'am. Mr. Sennett sent me."

"Mason?" Again her impulse was to glance at Gabriel to see if she could tell what he made of that. "Is something wrong?"

"Oh, no, ma'am. I was passing through the area and, knowing I would be, he asked me to stop by and see how you were getting along. He said he hadn't heard from you in a while."

"He's so thoughtful," she replied, touching a hand to her heart. If she pulled this off, she mused, she could try out for the thespian club over in Gatlinburg. "But what a worrywart. I've just been busy at school, that's all. You know, year-end exams?''

"Mr. Sennett thought it might be something like that. But he also wanted me to drop off a package for you. I left it on your patio table."

Glancing around him, Lisa spotted the beautifully gift-wrapped box. ''Oh, isn't that lovely? Why, only a minute ago I was telling Mr. Ballesteros how fortunate I've been to have such kind people helping me out.''

The man shifted his gaze once again to Gabriel. "Have we met before?"

"I doubt it,'' Lisa said quickly before Gabriel could reply. "Our church is sponsoring Mr. Ballesteros and he only arrived in the States a few weeks ago. I've hired him to help me around here. As you can see, I'm in the midst of some major repair work.''

She turned toward Gabriel and had to struggle to ignore the temper and warning she saw glinting in his eye. "Can we discuss painting later? You were absolutely right—I'm going to need more information about waterproofing and color availability before I can make an intelligent decision.''

Gabriel nodded. Barely. It was obvious by his rigid stance that he was furious with her, but she managed to turn back to Mason Sennett's messenger and give him a beaming smile.

"Why don't we go inside, Mr. Talbert, and I'll make you a glass of my herbal tea? Have you ever had it iced? Come along, Pilot. It's so soothing on the nerves. Or perhaps you'd prefer something stronger?''

"Plain water would be fine, ma'am.'' With a parting look and cursory nod toward Gabriel, the man called Talbert followed her to the house.

*   *   *

All his passion toward Lisa had always been giving, generous, but as Gabriel watched her enter the house with Sennett's young agent, he'd never been more tempted to throttle her. He swore under his breath and his blood did a slow seethe. What had she been thinking, pulling that employer-employee act? What was she trying to prove by taking a stranger into her home?

She's trying to protect you.

Hell, he thought clenching and unclenching his fists. Since when did the civilian protect the soldier? Since when did the novice ignore the warnings of the veteran? He didn't give a damn how archaic she might think it sounded, but he, who'd worked so hard to keep her removed from the ugliness and danger of his work, believed it was *his* responsibility to keep *her* safe.

Well, they were going to get a few things straight. He wouldn't stand for this happening again. He handled his own problems and got himself out of his own messes. If she didn't like it, tough.

It was only minutes later, after he'd showered the dust and sweat from his body and pulled on a clean pair of jeans and a shirt, that he discreetly rounded the back of his cottage and covertly made his way toward the house.

He checked the front first and spotted Talbert just leaving. His car was a nondescript blue sedan that he'd parked behind Lisa's vehicle. Rental, Gabriel thought searching for and noting the company's sticker. That made him feel slightly better. The story about Sennett's being concerned was probably true for the most part, and they weren't being put under any steady surveillance. But it still didn't excuse the risks Lisa had taken.

As he spotted Pilot following the agent out, Gabriel quickly made his way back to the patio and let himself in through the glass door. Lisa was waving goodbye, smiling like a model in a toothpaste commercial. But the instant she shut the door, the smile vanished. With a sigh, she leaned her forehead against the doorjamb.

"If it was that bad, you shouldn't have insisted on handling him on your own."

With a startled cry, she spun around. "How do you *do* that?" she gasped, pressing a hand to her chest.

He ignored the question and wandered farther into the room looking for telltale signs of where they'd sat. There were no glasses on the coffee table; Talbert hadn't gotten cozy with his wife on the couch. Good. He finally spotted them on the dinette table. That appeased his jealousy, until he remembered the time he and Lisa had once discovered brief but exquisite oblivion on the dinette table in their Alexandria apartment.

"So what did he want?" he demanded, shoving his hands into his jeans pockets and turning back to Lisa.

"Exactly what he said, I suppose. To... to check on me and deliver this." She crossed over to the bar that separated the living room from the kitchen and picked up a crystal vase from a deep box. "Isn't it lovely?"

"Sennett always did have expensive taste." Secretly, however, Gabriel thought the thing appeared as cold and empty as his life had seemed during his time away from her. How much better the vase would look if it was filled with white orchids to complement her creamy complexion. "But that doesn't answer my question. What did you and Talbert talk about?"

"Nothing of consequence."

"You mean you discussed the weather all that time?"

Lisa carefully returned the vase to the box before turning to face him. "I understand now. You're annoyed with me."

"Well, at least you haven't lost all your discerning facilities."

"And what is that supposed to mean?"

"What idiocy were you thinking when you invited him in here?"

"Oh, for goodness' sake, you make it sound as though I was in danger of being attacked or something."

"You find the possibility inconceivable?"

"The man was a perfect gentleman."

"Because this time his job called for him to look and act like one!"

Lisa lifted her chin. "If you thought he was that dangerous, then why did you let me get away with this?"

"What choice did I have? Before I knew what you were up to, you were already neck deep in your Scarlett O'Hara act." He knew he was sounding irrational and he paused to take a controlling breath. "All right . . . I was confident he didn't pose any danger to you," he began again. "But I want you to promise me you'll never pull a stunt like that again."

"What was I supposed to do? Let him stand out there and ask you a million and one questions? You heard him—he'd already thought maybe he'd met you before."

"That was just his way of fishing and you would have realized that if you hadn't been so eager to play spy yourself."

"Play..." Lisa's face turned beet red, and her eyes blazed. "He left, didn't he? *And* without any information."

"Little fool," Gabriel muttered, stepping toward her. "Don't you realize he didn't need to ask you anything? He needed to look around outside and in here. Did you leave him alone for any length of time?"

"What? N-no, of course not."

"Good, at least that's something. Wait a minute, was the front door unlocked? He could have slipped in here first before circling the house to come speak to us."

"No, I always lock it behind me. Only the back door was open." She shook her head in confusion. "Are you saying he wanted to plant a bug or something in here?"

"He could have."

"That's ridiculous. Why?"

"Because people like Talbert and especially Sennett are trained to be suspicious. That's what keeps them alive."

"I don't believe it. I won't. Mason invited me into his home. He put his children in my arms."

"Which proves he felt sorry for you and even liked you, but it doesn't discount the fact that you were the wife of one of his key people. Trust me, he would have this place bugged if he thought it was worth his while."

Lisa shook her head and backed a step away from him. "You should hear yourself. He was your friend, too. He was devastated when he thought you were dead. How can you believe—"

"Because I *think* like he does!" Gabriel ground out, not wanting to hear the rest. As much as this was hurting her, as much as it pained him, he needed to frighten her to make her understand this wasn't a game. "Grow up, Lisa. Chances are you've been watched from the moment they told you I was missing. Your phones were undoubtedly tapped, your credit files inspected. Do you have any idea how much information can be gleaned from them alone? Within hours they probably knew things about you that would make you blush.''

''Why would they bother?''

''They could never *prove* I was dead. No matter what they said to you, they knew what that could mean, and you represented their best chance for information if there were any.''

''You sound as though you approve of that.''

''In a way I do, because back then there could have been people far more dangerous to you searching, as well, and I'm glad to think Sennett's men would have been there if the wrong person had found you.''

Lisa hugged herself as if cold and shook her head in rejection of that. ''Talbert came to deliver an early birthday present and that's all,'' she insisted, her voice growing more unsteady with each second. ''Why must you reduce everything to subterfuge? Why must you denounce everyone's kindness to me as malevolent or having an ulterior motive?''

He could see she was near tears and the knowledge cut him, but he could also see he hadn't quite convinced her. ''Because this isn't the safe nice world you try to pretend it is,'' he rasped. ''There isn't anything more dangerous or dirty than the world I worked in. There are people out there who speak politely and look congenial but who would kill at the drop of a hat if the order came to do so. Remember that, Lisa. Remember what I was next time you're tempted to stand between me and a man wearing a gun.''

''Oh, don't!'' She clasped her hands over her ears. ''I don't want to hear any more.''

He crossed the room and took hold of her wrists. The slightness of her bones made him ache; he'd snapped wrists twice as strong. "Lisa, *querida*, listen."

"No! No more," she cried. "I can't." Her voice broke on a sob and she tried to duck her head and hide her tears from him. "I can't take any more of this."

"I'm only trying to make you see reality."

"I don't want any part of your reality. I want my life back. I want my sanity back. Oh, God, I wish I'd never met you!"

She was killing him. Like a frantic bird struggling from captivity, she fought his hold. The first heavy tears spilling from her lashes matched the drops of blood he was certain were dripping from the wound in his heart. "Ah, no," he entreated, bending to kiss her. "Don't say such things. You know you don't mean them."

But the way she was resisting him indicated otherwise until, finally, he was forced to use a greater strength. Shifting his hold, he trapped her tightly against him. The shudder that racked her body was as grievous to him as her bitter words, and he was almost relieved when she buried her face against his shoulder and let her tears spill freely.

"Lisa . . ." He whispered her name like a prayer, just as he'd done in his darkest moments, and pressed random soothing kisses to the top of her head, first to one feverish temple, and then the other. He knew he had no right to take any pleasure from the act—should only give comfort—and yet he did, *he did*. Holding her like this was a gift he would have paid nearly any price to achieve. He couldn't stop stroking her hair or her back, nor could he resist spreading more kisses wherever he could touch her.

He wasn't consciously aware of when those kisses changed, when they went from soothing to hungry, just as he wasn't immediately aware of when her hands began their own journey over him or when she parted her lips to him. But suddenly it was happening—they were caught in the dizzying whirlpool of an all-consuming kiss.

Gabriel crushed her closer. How long had it been? How many times had he dreamed of having her like this? A lifetime. Eternity. He tried to temper it to something more gentle, but his soul was starving. When he felt her blindly push the shirt he'd never bothered to button over his shoulders, desperation possessed him.

Letting the shirt slide to the floor, he drew back her head and stared down into her tear and passion-glazed eyes. "I need you," he groaned hoarsely.

She started like someone jerked from a deep sleep and went as cold and still as death. The fear of rejection swept through him faster than a blast of January air on a Washington, D.C., street corner, and as she removed her hands from his shoulders and he watched her curl those craved-for fingers into fists that made her nails bite fiercely into the tender flesh of her palms, he felt abysmally empty and lost.

His heart pounded against his ribs as destructively as the sledgehammer he'd used earlier. It couldn't end here; he wanted to sweep her into his arms and carry her to her bedroom, their bed. He wanted to love her. But he also knew that would be impossible if it wasn't what she wanted, too.

He stepped away from her, extended his hand and waited. Seconds. A lifetime. And nothing happened.

He closed his eyes nearly to the point of wishing he'd been consumed by those flames in Argentina, because he knew her rejection now was going to be more than he could bear. But he wouldn't beg. If he was to survive at all, he couldn't beg.

Just as he began to lower his hand, he felt her fingertips, fluttering like the heartbeat of a sparrow. They inched over his callused palm until finally coming to rest.

He closed his fingers around hers as though grasping a lifeline.

Seven

Muted light filtered in through the bedroom's drawn blue-and-mauve-patterned draperies creating a shadowy environment where whispers seemed compulsory and Lisa's berry-and-amber fragrance hovered like a discreet caress. Though Gabriel had thus far only allowed himself the luxury of trespassing here once, for days now this was where his thoughts had dwelled. Like a returning exile, he walked into the room, sucked her haunting velvet-soft scent deep into his lungs and possessively eyed the antique four-poster they had shared in Virginia.

But most of all he focused on Lisa, who lowered herself onto the edge of the bed as if her legs would no longer carry her. The way she gripped the carved bedpost made him wonder if she wasn't preparing herself more for the onslaught of a tidal wave. On the other hand maybe that was wise, for right now he felt as dangerous and combustible as any violent storm, and like a drenching downpour, he wanted to be all over her.

She looked surreal, a memory he'd never let die, a phantasm he prayed would not evaporate when he reached out for her. He'd read somewhere that the eye loved novelty. It was true, he thought, staring at the picture she made. Sitting on the bedspread that matched the draperies, she looked like an exotic water lily floating on a midnight pool whose moonlit surface shimmered like sapphires and amethysts.

Over the past few years, when the pain became too much to bear or his desolation too overwhelming to champion, he would dream of seeing her this way. But the woman he approached, whose silken hair he stroked and whose trembling fingers slowly traced a sensuous path up his bare arm to cling to his shoulder, was no figment. Just like his, her pulse was racing at a feverish pace.

Need, hunger, *desire,* those human feelings woke him from his dazed state. At least he recovered enough to shakily exhale his pent-up breath, steady himself by resting one knee on the bed and claim the lips she offered with the reverence of a flower reaching for the first droplet of rain.

He had always loved kissing Lisa, loved turning it into a languid journey of feasting and discovery. She had such tastes, a lush yet subdued elegance reminiscent of a particular Rioja wine he'd experienced in a Spanish bodega. And she was a constant surprise—soft, yet possessing a surprising undercurrent of strength that, mingled with her liquid heat, entranced and seduced him as nothing and no one had before or since.

He used the tip of his tongue to caress the outer perimeters of her mouth and savor the more fragile essence of her before tenderly suckling her lower lip to signal he was ready to journey deeper. Her soft utterance of pleasure and welcome wafted over him, insulating his sense of rightness so that when he finally penetrated the warm haven of her mouth, he did it with a fierce tenderness that promised this was only the beginning.

The kiss went on and on, not entirely patient, yet without the frantic rush of previous kisses. Finally, by some mutual but unspoken agreement he lifted his head. As much as he wanted to kiss her, what he wanted more was to see the effect of their passion on her face and in her eyes. Lisa's sexual honesty had always been as gratifying as it was humbling, and spotting it now, the naked invitation that illuminated her gray eyes with a near phosphorescent shimmering, gave him the impetus, the *right* to lower her back onto the bed.

Skin and clothing whispered with their movements and were echoed by their mutual sighs. "*Dios,* it almost hurts," he rasped, sharply aware of how long it had been since they'd been together like this. Wondering whether he could keep himself under control long enough to please her, he swept his gaze over the hair cascading across his arm and onto the bedspread. He drew his free hand down to her hip and brought her into a more intimate and perfect alignment with his own body. "Yet you feel like heaven."

"I've been afraid to admit how much I miss this."

Her barely audible admission brought him as much pleasure as the bite of her short nails into his biceps or the restless flurry of kisses she traced along one shoulder. Awarding a more ardent but equally careful nibble to the tempting side of her neck, he asked, "Tell me. Tell me what you've missed."

"The way you make me feel, first with a look, a kiss, then with your hands and body." In response he shaped the rounded curve of her hip, pressing himself more intimately into her softness, which had her briefly biting her lower lip. "That," she acknowledged, her voice turning reedy. "The way you reduce me to a creature of sensation waiting impatiently for the next lesson you'll teach me."

"It's not just sensation."

"It would be so much easier if it were."

Her words were a tiny cloud marring his panorama, a gust of north wind chilling his summery mood, a shadow of foreboding on the horizon of his happiness. With grim determination, he raised himself over her, gripping her wrists and pressing her hands deeper into the bedding at each side of her head.

"It's not just sensation," he repeated with gritty authority before crushing his mouth to hers.

This time his kiss was less careful and less patient. A whisper of desperation had touched his heart and he needed to purge it. Thrusting his tongue deeply into her mouth and showing her with a thoroughly carnal stroking how he would claim her with his body, he released one of her wrists to seek her breast.

Her soft moan was a balm to his hurt; her subtle arching into the pressure he exuded with his palm kindled an even greater desire for her. Trailing a series of hot kisses across her cheek and down her throat, he came to the V-neckline of her blouse and began to release one button after the other.

Beneath the demure but feminine blouse was more silk in a matching color. It resembled a confection more than clothing, the kind he'd fantasized about for more than a thousand nights. He drew off her blouse and then the matching camisole, exploring and tasting the sleek warm skin he exposed until he had her down to her bra.

Definitely confection, he decided, admiring the wispy garment. He wanted to smile, to tell her it was wonderful, that *she* was wonderful; but anticipation was sharpening to something more closely resembling torment. After only a fleeting caress with the backs of his fingers over one delicate lace-covered breast, he released the bra's front clasp and brushed aside the scrap of lavender temptation.

His gaze worshiped, his touch cherished. Tracing the small but perfect shape of her, the already taut peak, exquisitely pink like the protected center of a seashell, he was once again assaulted by memories of how she liked to be touched and the sounds he could draw from her. Driven by the desire to please as much as a wholly masculine need to hear those sounds again, he lowered his head to her.

At the first brush of his lips, he heard her gasp; when he explored her with his tongue, she writhed beneath him in sensual torment. And when he finally, hungrily, drew her into his mouth, she gripped handfuls of his hair and uttered a whimpering moan. He understood only too well the strange mixture of pain and pleasure that reverberated in her voice and shook her body. After having practically convinced himself that he would never touch her in this way again, his own joy was almost too much to bear.

It was the reflexive twist of her torso, the way she drew her leg up and along his to hold him closer that snapped the lingering threads of his control. Muttering something that could have been her name or a plea, he once again crushed his mouth to hers while sliding his hand beneath her, making short work of her skirt's button and zipper. As he peeled off her remaining clothes, he covered every inch of newly exposed skin with hot kisses.

When he dropped the last scrap of lingerie to the floor and bent to nip the inside of her thigh, Lisa shuddered and twisted out of his reach. "No more," she pleaded, one arm flung across her eyes. "I can't... I don't think..."

"Shh. Don't think," he replied, rising from the bed just long enough to strip off his jeans. Once again with her, he smoothed her hair, made a place for himself between her legs. "Don't think. Just feel...me... you...us."

With each word he kissed her, skimmed his fingers along her thighs, explored the moist hot intimate place he longed to bury himself. Which one of them moaned? He didn't know. He only knew his skin felt as though it was blistering and if he didn't have her soon... Lifting his desperate gaze to hers, he found her watching him. Her skin was as slick as his, her eyes as feverish.

"Lisa..."

"Do it," she entreated.

Slowly he began to enter her. She was ready for him and yet he took care, mindful that it had been a long time and that she had always fit him like a glove. Once he felt himself sheathed in hot wet satin, his body screamed to initiate that age-old rhythm that would give him the relief he'd been convinced he would never know again, but he forced himself to remain still and silent. Lisa, on the other hand, reacted with a strangled thoroughly erotic sound.

"What?" he prompted hoarsely.

"I thought..."

He watched as she had to swallow and moisten her lips. Greedily wanting even that sweetness, he swooped down and licked it away. "What? What did you think?"

"That I'd never feel like this again."

"Yes," he whispered. "Tell me how do you feel."

"Alive. Whole."

He, too, was pulsating with life and experiencing that full-to-overflowing sensation. "And?"

"Possessed."

"You are. You always were, even when I wasn't with you. It's the same way with me."

"It's insane."

Once again that note of doubt had crept back into her voice. "It's reality," he muttered, thrusting deeper into her. "Reality," he groaned again, crushing his lips to hers for another feverish kiss.

With his mouth and his body he urged her into accepting, surrendering, losing herself in him. The pace was slow but intense. One by one he felt the walls she'd been building between them since his return come crashing down, until she was answering his body's demands with her own, until she was biting back cries of pleasure.

Still, he sensed some corner of her withholding herself. It hurt and it frightened him. But more than anything he felt angry as hell. Only the awareness of his own impending completion forced him to accept there could be no contest of wills this time.

Intensifying his thrusts, he raced her to the brink and watched her pleasure through passion-glazed eyes. He was painfully aware that only in the last instant did she willingly cling to him. Yet, ravaged soul that he was, it was enough to incite his own shuddering climax.

* * *

Beneath her damp skin, her nerve endings hummed, her muscles protested, her bones ached. Even the roots of her hair felt as though they'd been under some sort of siege. She never wanted to open her eyes again, but not because she was tired. She was also afraid. The worst of it was she deserved to be.

This shouldn't have happened, she told herself before a last rippling ghost of a spasm coursed through her body. And it was her fault that it had. From the beginning she'd been aware of the risk she would be taking if she wasn't careful, if she let down her guard. It wasn't that she didn't want him; dear Lord, she thought, feeling him draw a deep breath beside her, he'd just proven she did with humbling clarity. She would always want him; however, that didn't mean she should have given in to that desire and made love with him. He was going to take it the wrong way, read permanency and acceptance where there should have been only longing and resignation. Of that she was certain.

What was he going to say when she tried to explain? She dreaded just thinking about it; at the least he was going to be hurt. At the worst...

"You're very quiet."

She wasn't fooled by his calm tone. He was far too peremptory these days to pull that off convincingly. On the other hand, shouting matches weren't his style, either. Still, she had no doubt he'd reflected over and analyzed what had just happened and was intent on discussing his comprehensive and probably accurate conclusions just to prove a point. Would she, she wondered, be as quietly resigned when he was through?

"So are you," she replied cautiously.

He turned to her and rose on one elbow. The heat of his gaze alone, as it slid over her, rekindled her awareness; when he drew his finger in a serpentine path down the center of her body, it was all she could do not to moan aloud.

"Me, I was counting."

As his finger circled her navel, she felt her abdominal and leg muscles contract in anticipation. "Counting what?"

"Minutes—or however long it will take for you to start telling me this was a mistake."

How could she focus on what he was saying when he was looking at her as though she was the most delectable French pastry and he was a man who'd come off a long fast? It was incredible; here she should be feeling... The word *embarrassed* came to mind, but that wasn't exactly right. Disturbed. Disturbed over the reckless haste with which they'd ended up in bed together. Instead, however, she couldn't get past her sexual awareness, the rekindling of her desire for him.

She closed her eyes and tried to concentrate. "It was inevitable. I can accept that much."

"Inevitable. What isn't between us?"

That made her eyes whip open, but she immediately realized it had been a trick. While his words had been spoken laconically, his gaze exposed a fury that tempted her to seek cover. Of course, she knew better than to believe he would allow her to even budge at this point. "You're going to make me say it, aren't you?"

"Yes." The word was drawn out in the same way he prolonged the slow navigation of his long fingers around the circumference of her right breast. Lisa could feel her skin tingle, her nipple bead in reaction and expectancy of more. "I want us to be perfectly clear about our expectations, so neither of us will misunderstand the other."

"Please don't be bitter. It wasn't my intention to upset you."

"But you have. Do you think two people who have shared the intimacies we have can hide what they're truly feeling from one another, even after a long absence?" His voice shook with suppressed emotion, yet his touch was astonishingly gentle as he brushed his knuckles across the peak of her breast. "A few minutes ago you held back part of yourself, part of your response to me. You let me have your body, but you kept the deepest part of yourself, your heart, detached. In doing so, you not only cheated me, you were being dishonest to yourself."

Ashamed that he could see through her so easily, Lisa wished for the first time she had the nerve to drag the bedspread around her to at least hide her nakedness; it was humiliating enough that he was seeing the secrets of her mind. "I was afraid," she admitted slowly.

"Of me?"

"Partly."

"Of the way I look?"

"*No.*" Her hoarse whisper held as much despair as his did when he'd posed his question. It pained her to think he could still be torturing himself over her feelings about his injuries. Immediately dismissing whatever else she was going to say to him, she rose to her knees and unhesitatingly laid her hand against the left side of his face, touched her lips to his brow, awarded another kiss to the black patch covering his eye, and yet another to the scar running along his jaw to beneath his ear. "Never, never think that again. I can't bear it. I can't—" Her voice broke on a sob.

"Ssh..." He grabbed her hand and fervently pressed his lips into her palm. "It's all right," he assured her, keeping her hand imprisoned in his and using his other hand to stroke her hair. "It doesn't matter."

"Of course, it matters."

"Then I believe you."

"You're just saying that to make me feel better."

He laughed then, a laugh that held more irony than humor, and lowered his head until his forehead touched hers. "By all that's holy, I wish I knew the secret to erase all these doubts and insecurities between us, and... Ah, *querida,* how am I supposed to stay angry with you when you turn me inside out like this?"

"I don't want you to be angry, I want you to understand that I need some time and space to come to terms with things."

"Part of marriage is two people 'coming to terms with things,'" he reminded her gently.

"Really? Is that why you took three years to come back to me?" Lisa lowered her eyes to her wedding band. "I don't believe you ever took us—me—seriously."

"How can you say that?" he ground out, gripping her shoulders so tightly she winced.

"It's what I feel. You didn't respect me or our relationship enough to treat me as an equal. Don't misunderstand, at first I loved the feeling of being cherished. But then I realized what you were really doing is treating me like a doll you could take down from a shelf and play with for a while, only to put me back up there out of the way when it was time to deal with serious things." She shook her head at herself. "It didn't even begin to register until just before you left on your last trip and then I tried to convince myself otherwise. I can't let you

do that to me again. Something inside me would wither
and die.''

Tears of regret over opportunities missed burned in
her eyes, and she even felt a touch of anxiety because
she couldn't tell by his closed expression what he was
thinking, or how he was going to react to what
amounted to being told there were still emotional roadblocks between them. She wasn't entirely surprised to
hear the raggedly-whispered oath, but what she didn't
expect was once again to be pressed back against the
mattress and kissed with a desperate yet tender fer-
vency until she had to beg him for air.

''I can't change the past,'' he told her, sweeping his
hand down the length of her and back again, reminding her that there wasn't an inch of her he wasn't acutely
intimate with. ''And I can't make you stop believing
what you want to believe. But you were never a play-
thing to me. You were my salvation, and I'd challenge
any man to deny he would do whatever necessary to
protect what he cherished the most. What's more, you
do know me. You know how to make me crazy, and you
know how badly I want you. You know that I couldn't
stay away, and that I have no intention of leaving you
again.''

''Do I?''

''Yes, damn it!'' He pressed an ardent kiss against
the side of her neck, then another. ''Lisa . . . Lisa, you
learned things about me that shocked and upset you.
You'll undoubtedly learn more in the future, but what
I can only tell you is that I was a different better man
with you. No one and nothing is going to take that away
from me.'' He raised his head slightly to gaze deeply
into her eyes. ''I'll try to be patient, to wait for you to
give me the words I know are in your heart, but as for

the rest... Ask me to give up breathing—it would be easier.''

His next kiss was hard, immediately demanding. His tongue pierced deep, unequivocally staking claim. Heat flared and not unlike a match touched to a stack of dried hay exploded into an inferno. It shocked Lisa, who'd believed she wouldn't be as vulnerable to him a second time. It only proved how much she had yet to learn about herself, how much she had underestimated his power over her and how intense and deep their passion burned.

Knowing that by giving in she would be making a mockery of everything she'd just said to him, she tried to twist away, to speak. But he kept her imprisoned with his body, and he absorbed her protests with fervent kisses, until she felt as though he was trying to absorb her into himself.

She would have to be dead not to respond; he would have to be someone other than who he was for her to keep resisting him. With her hand fluttering unsteadily against his cheek, an action that exposed her inner trauma, she accepted the return of his mouth to hers and curled her tongue around his, intensifying the intimate stroking into a mutual sharing.

Touched by his groan of pleasure, she abandoned her attempt to push against his chest and reached up to spear her fingers into his long hair. Caught in something profound and inescapable, she could only reach toward it.

"Touch me," he said. "Like that... yes... I want to feel your hands. I want them... all over me.''

She slid them down his back massaging lean corded muscles, exploring the breadth of his shoulders, down past his trim waist to his athletically taut buttocks. As he murmured his encouragement, she continued her journey upward to the dark forest of hair matting his chest, beneath which his heart pounded as fierce as a train engine racing toward some impossible destination. His nipples were hard and, she soon realized, unbearably sensitive. At the first scrape of her nails he sucked in his breath, prompting her to repeat the caress. If she'd never discovered his true identity any other way, she thought, she would probably have recognized him this way, through his receptivity to her. This is what they had in common, an equal insatiable sexual attraction for one another. It wasn't enough, but right now he was proving how impossible it was to ignore.

"Tell me you don't want this," he rasped, sliding his mouth down her body to nip at the sensitive indentation of her waist, then kiss the damp skin just below her navel. "Tell me you want me to stop." He never stayed still, touching her everywhere except her breasts and when she thought she was going to scream if he deprived them of his attention a moment longer, she felt the heat of his breath there. "Tell me," he demanded.

"Please. Don't tease me."

"Does it hurt?"

"You know it does."

"How badly?"

"Like someone's tearing off my skin strip by strip."

"Then you know how it feels when you try to deny me and our feelings for one another." He closed his mouth over one breast, appeased the first wave of hunger and then administered to the other. "Don't try to deny us this again, *querida*. You'll only lose."

With that he surged into her. Lisa felt the power of it, the sensation of being completely filled shoot to every nerve ending in her body. Helpless not to, she drew him closer and reached for the oblivion she knew only he could bring her.

Eight

"**I** was thinking of planting a redbud tree here...."

Gabriel looked up from the nuts and bolts he was securing on the new porch swing to watch Lisa step back several yards from the second cottage's front porch and point to a bare spot of earth to the left of the steps. Instead of analyzing her suggestion, he admired the picture she made dressed in khaki shorts and a coffee-brown T-shirt with her long hair tied back from her face by a gold-and-rust print scarf. She looked like a sparrow, inquisitive and energetic as she visualized how the area would ultimately look when everything was done.

"...and forsythia bushes at both corners of the cottage to add a contrast to the azaleas in between. What do you think?" she asked, glancing over at him.

"It depends." He returned his attention to his work, giving the nut a final twist. "Am I going to be drafted as the official hole digger?"

"Such enthusiasm. No, I can manage perfectly on my own, thank you."

The mock hauteur in her voice had him grinning and feeling something as poignantly close to happiness as he dared allow at this point. Of course, he was too aware of the metaphorical mine fields lurking beneath this fragile serenity to allow himself to relax completely.

In the two days since school had been dismissed for summer break, they'd been working side by side from practically dawn to dusk. He'd been looking forward to that since his arrival, having her completely to himself for hours, the opportunity to reminisce, to talk about her future plans for the place and to simply look at her. But little did she know that along with his anticipation was an angst he'd never even experienced as a teenager about to "do it" for the first time.

As a result, the rapport they were sharing today hadn't been an effortless accomplishment. In many respects Lisa had been right about him; he was a private man and there would always be a side of himself, things in his past, he would unequivocally find difficult to share.

Only a few days ago he'd offended her by avoiding a question she'd posed to him about the term "trouble-shooter" as it applied to covert government work. Specifically, she'd asked if the process still involved finely negotiated diplomacy or if it was less civilized. Gabriel knew what was behind the question: it had finally struck her that he might be like those men he'd talked about, that he might have had the occasion to take a life. He hadn't begrudged her her curiosity—actually, he was surprised the subject hadn't come up sooner—but was he willing to answer it? He'd concluded he would more willingly face a full congressional hearing than admit or deny anything when it was impossible for him to explain in full detail. So, he replied only that the ambiguity of the term ran a direct parallel to the work itself.

She made no comment to that and yet he felt as though an invisible mark was drawn against him. The question was, how many was he allowed in this equally ambiguous contest of wills?

He was already paying a price; she was carefully avoiding any intimacy that would precipitate in a recurrence of the lovemaking they'd shared several days ago. His dove, he mused, had grown talons. As an intensely sensual man with a discriminating appetite for only one woman, she'd expertly, maddeningly, retaliated where he would suffer most.

And yet the tide hadn't turned completely against him; already there had been several instances where *she* had been the one who'd been left struggling to contain her deeper feelings. Finding a middle ground on which to communicate might leave them, more often than not, juggling an emotional powder keg, but it was also proving delightfully illuminating.

Making love, however, didn't seem to be on her mind at the moment and, with a philosophical sigh, he pushed himself to his feet and joined her. "Twelve acres of trees and she wants to plant more," he drawled under his breath, brushing his hands against his jeans.

"It's not the same. Most of these native trees don't bloom."

"Ah, so that's the criterion. Well, why didn't you say so?" Narrowing his eye and stroking his jaw, he pretended to visualize her plan. "Breathtaking," he concluded. "Shall I get you the shovel?"

"All right, I get the hint. Let's take a break." She stripped off the gardening gloves she'd been wearing while weeding and tying down the daffodil greens so they wouldn't look messy as they absorbed nutrients for next spring's blooms.

"I have a better idea," Gabriel said as he caught her arm before she could sit down on a nearby rock. "Let's hang the swing and then we can test it while we're resting."

"Now who's being a slave driver?"

"Practical thinker." He indicated the ant colony near where she'd planned to sit. "You'd only have to move again, anyway."

Together they lifted the wooden swing and the accompanying yards of chain and carried it onto the new porch that Gabriel had completed only the other day. Balancing the bulk of the swing on a railing, he climbed the stepladder and secured first one chain and then the other to the hooks he'd already screwed into overhead beams.

"That looks about the right height to me. What do you think?" he asked, trying to gauge the position of the swing to the deck.

"It's perfect—if you have the legs of an ostrich." Sitting down, Lisa swung her feet showing him how they cleared the ground by at least a half a foot.

He shook the chain to chase her off. Muttering about too many chiefs and not enough Indians, he readjusted it. "There. Now try it."

Lisa did and sighed contentedly. "Lovely. Now if only someone would ring for the servants to fetch lunch and something cool to drink."

Without comment, Gabriel descended the ladder and opened the cottage's screen door, then pulled out a small ice chest. The contents yielded two plastic cups and an iced bottle of water. "I can't help you with the food, but this should quench your thirst."

"You angel."

Though his answering smile was skeptical, there was no denying that inside he felt a surge of pleasure. "Now there's a first. Usually I've been called things on the other end of the spectrum."

"Maybe because you don't let anyone get close enough to you to give them more opportunities to see this side of you," she replied, focusing on the cup he handed her.

"Considering my business, it would hardly have been wise." He filled her cup and then his own before setting aside the bottle.

"Yet you broke your own rules when I came along."

"When you came along," he murmured, before taking a long drink. He couldn't help but wonder where this odd conversation was leading. "Yes. But then you were never business." More like a complication, he thought wryly.

Lisa seemed to chew over that for a moment. "Why?" she asked suddenly. "I mean what was it about me that made you go against your natural inclination?" His expression must have mirrored his incredulity for she gestured to him to wait and let her explain. "When I was younger I used to love to read Regency romances, you know the kind where—"

"There's little more physical contact than an ardent kiss on the last page? I read a few myself," he said, shrugging at her look of astonishment.

"*When?*"

"A lifetime ago. I was just starting out, guarding someone in a safe house. There was nothing to do and I'd noticed there was a used-book store in the shopping center behind us that left bags and boxes of books out by the garbage receptacles. You know the kind with the covers torn off and generally in bad shape? I would sneak out and grab a few. They were a mix of other things, too, but I read them all. Even the romances."

Resting her elbow on her upraised knee, Lisa nibbled at her thumbnail. Her eyes took on a decided twinkle. "Talk about unbelievable scenarios."

"Enjoy yourself... only remember when you're screaming for mercy that I know all your ticklish spots," he warned, already looking forward to the prospect of exacting retribution.

She cleared her throat and straightened to a more conservative position.

"Finish your story," he prodded more gently.

For a moment he thought she was going to refuse, but then she shrugged. "What I was going to say was that I'd always had difficulty with the heroine asking the hero, 'why me?' after the hero declared he's in love with her. It always seemed... I guess a good word would be feigning. But now, knowing how improbable it was for us to have... Well, I realize it's the same question I've wanted to ask you."

And one Gabriel had no problem summoning an answer to. "You were innocent," he said simply. "It made me feel... clean... new. Like I was being given a second chance in life. And you made me feel as though I was building toward something constructive. For someone in my business where progress is often at best a lateral shifting of powers, you can't imagine how refreshing that was."

"I could try if you'd explain it to me."

Gabriel smiled sadly. "Sometimes I have a difficult time understanding it myself. But I'll tell you this—strange things happen to a man when he approaches his middle years. He's passed the nonsense of believing he's superman and he begins to realize his life is mounted on well-greased roller skates. In a blink of an eye he's going to be old, dead. He starts to look around him, gauging what he's accomplished thus far. It didn't take me long to realize that my life's accomplishments didn't amount to the flicker of a firefly's fragile light. Then I met you," he added quietly, "and I spotted an intangible something I'd never allowed myself to dwell on before."

"What?"

"The love that my parents had shared."

Lisa's expression turned tender. "Tell me. I always thought... The way you rarely spoke of them, I thought it wasn't a good marriage."

"In many ways it wasn't. My father was away from home too much. But now you can understand where I came by my restless nature," he told her wryly. "He had an inherent curiosity about the world, a need for adventure and challenge. He was a professional soldier. That's a more genteel way of saying he was a mercenary," he explained when he noticed her quizzical expression.

"And your mother? You told me once she was born in Spain, but you never elaborated."

"She was the daughter of an artist. Very romantic, like you. Very idealistic. She and my father met when he was between wars. My father saw her through the window of the New York art gallery where her father was having an exclusive showing. He crashed the private party and somehow convinced her to meet him for a drink later that night. They were married a short time later."

"Like us," Lisa whispered, her eyes softening to something so inviting that Gabriel felt himself pulled, drowning.

"Like us. Only my mother paid an immediate price for her impetuousness. Her father disowned her. It wasn't too bad in the beginning," he added quickly at Lisa's hushed gasp. "They were too crazy about each other to notice they had almost nothing in common and were almost paupers. Then my mother got pregnant and reality set in. Try as he did, my father wasn't able to handle a regular job, nor was he cut out for routines or children. So he went back to his wars. This time it was Cambodia."

"And your mother waited?"

"Always. We had a swing not unlike this one and I remember her sitting here at the end of the day, reading and rereading his letters until it was too dark to see. Then the letters stopped coming. After a while a telegram did. She was never the same after that. It was as if a part of her had died with him. She started daydreaming a lot. One day while in town doing her shopping, she stepped in front of a truck. There was a time I wanted to hate her because I thought she'd done it on purpose. I wish I could tell her that I understand now."

Lisa offered no words of sympathy, but simply laid her head on his shoulder, which was something that touched him more deeply.

After a while she asked, "How old were you?"

"Sixteen. An old sixteen," he added before she could comment upon his youth. "It wasn't so bad, but I did miss her. Never so much as when I met you. God, I wanted her to meet you. She would have been pleased."

"Maybe she would have wanted you to marry a girl of her own culture."

"She would have wanted me to marry a lady, which I most definitely did."

"Did you ever get to meet your grandfather?"

Gabriel smiled, understanding that she'd been flattered but embarrassed by his compliment. Well, she would just have to get used to his compliments, he thought. "Yes. During my summer breaks in college, I went to Spain and stayed with him. He was an odd, lonely man, too rigid to forget the past, but wanting something from me that I never quite understood. We never became close exactly, but I kept visiting him whenever I could until he passed away."

"Those must have been happy times for him," Lisa said, and switched her glass to her other hand in order to lace her fingers with his. "Can I tell you something?"

"Only if it's flattering." He sensed she was about to say something profound and was instinctively protecting himself by using humor.

"I've never felt closer to you than at this moment. Thank you . . . for sharing."

Gabriel sighed. "They're just tattered memories, *querida*. They can do no one any good. They only make the heart sore, and mine already suffers enough whenever I look at your sweet face."

Through her hand he could feel her pulse flutter like a feather caught in an errant breeze. She shifted slightly to smile at him. "I think you inherited your gift for being disarmingly charming from your Spanish ancestors."

"Are you feeling disarmed, my dove?" he murmured, deciding that if he didn't kiss her soon he would go quietly, completely, out of his mind.

But just as he began to lower his head, Pilot leapt to his feet from his resting spot under a shade tree and started barking. "Damn it," he growled, seeing the woman who was walking toward them. "You would think living out here would guarantee one some decent privacy." Unlike him, however, Lisa seemed relieved to see their visitor.

"It's Marie. I've been wanting her to meet you."

It was bad enough that she might be disturbed at what the woman may or may not have seen, Gabriel thought grimly, but what added to his plunging spirits was feeling Lisa disengage her hand from his, then rise from the swing and put several safe yards between them.

"Have you?" he muttered. "Introducing one's *handyman* to friends must be a social etiquette I'm not yet familiar with."

"Gabriel..."

She shot him a hurt look, but Marie was already too close to say more. As her friend called something out to Lisa, she simply shook her head at him in a way that said, "You don't understand at all" and turned to focus on her guest.

"I can't believe how much you've done with the place," Marie said a while later as Lisa led her across the bridge to show her what she planned for the other cottages. "Oh, and look at all the flowers. No wonder you don't have time to go anywhere with me."

The midday sun filtering through a gnarled sweet gum showed off red, white and violet primroses against the elegant foilage of daylilies, which had yet to bloom.

Lisa tried to view the manicured scene and take satisfaction in it, but her mind kept returning to Gabriel. She wondered where he'd gone off to. After she'd introduced him to Marie, she'd invited him to join them as she showed her friend what had been accomplished over the past several weeks; however, he'd made some excuse about having to check on something and had disappeared.

"I don't blame you."

Lisa turned back to the outspoken brunette. "What?"

"If I were you, I'd be wondering where he'd vanished to myself. In fact, if I were you, I'd tell me to get lost and go find out."

"Oh, Marie," Lisa sighed.

"Don't go getting all puritan on me. I have a nose for chemistry."

"And an imagination for drama."

Though her friend dismissed that with the wave of coral-tipped fingers, she soon grew more serious. "It's so sad—his face, I mean. Has he talked about how it happened?"

"Not in any great detail," Lisa replied, leading the way to the third cabin. "It was a car accident, and a long time ago. He doesn't like to dwell on it."

"No, I guess he wouldn't. But mercy, Lisa, scars or not, the man's definitely got something."

"He's a nice man," she said neutrally, wondering how to change the subject without seeming too obvious.

But her reply earned her a look that would have popped Marie's contacts, if she'd been wearing them instead of her glasses. "Are you serious? *Nice?* Lisa, the old darling who delivers my mail is 'nice.' Mr. Thurman who grinds extra lean ground chuck for Daddy is 'nice.' Gabriel Ballesteros is . . . is . . .''

"Why do I get the feeling I'm about to be tempted to put my hands over my ears?'' Lisa drawled.

"...like Armagnac. Or something exotic that we girls are always tempted to order as an after-dinner drink but don't have the nerve, so we settle for a ladylike Amaretto.''

Lisa stopped dead in her tracks. "Marie, what are you talking about?''

"Gabriel. He's like the dark mysterious-looking guy who sits on the other side of a bar. We're dying to go talk to him, but instead we settle for the sweet safe guy who comes to talk to us.''

"Uh-huh. You forget I've seen you in action,'' Lisa said pointedly. "You've never been too shy to approach anyone.''

"There've been one or two who've given me weak knees. But we're not talking about me, dear heart. We're talking about you and your bronzed-for-posterity good-girl image. If you ask me, I think it's time you tucked it away along with your wedding ring and that invisible mourning shroud you're still hiding behind. *I* think it's time you noticed what took me only a second to see—that Gabriel looks at you the way someone in the Sahara would look at a double scoop of French vanilla ice cream.'' Marie lifted her hair off the back of her neck and daintily fanned herself. "**I** should have your opportunities.''

Her wistful comment was lost on Lisa, who hadn't gotten past Marie's analogy. It alone had her imagination running rampant and almost had her mimicking her friend's motions. Gabriel not only would *look*, he would kiss her as if she was melting ice cream, had in fact done that only days ago.

Torn between laughing and groaning at the craziness of it all, Lisa muttered, "You're decadent."

"Correction—bored. I've had it up to here with the safe men in this town," she said, drawing an imaginary line across her forehead. "And I'm equally fed up with my safe job and my safe life. I want *passion*, Lisa. That's why I recognize it when I see it. That man has the hots for you, and if you don't do something about it, you're crazy."

"You always think I'm crazy," Lisa replied, secretly wishing she could confide in Marie that she already had done something about it. But of course that was impossible. It would just encourage questions she was unable to answer. That hurt. Marie was a good friend; she deserved her honesty. Gabriel, however, needed her protection.

But what Marie's comment did offer was the chance to bring up a nagging worry that Lisa was willing and able to talk about. "What happens after the fireworks?" she challenged quietly. "I need more. I want a husband I can depend on to be there for me in the bad times as well as the good, or even in the ho-hum in-between times. I want children. I want stability, Marie. Passion isn't going to guarantee me that."

"Nothing is."

Frustrated, Lisa bent to pick up a rock, and she threw it toward the creek, which had Pilot taking off in hot pursuit. "You know what I mean."

"Okay, so in that case you'd need to take the Marie Thomas is-this-relationship-worth-pursuing test."

"I'll probably regret asking this, but what, pray tell, is that?"

"It's when you close your eyes and ask yourself, how would I feel if this person walked out of my life tomorrow? If you can shrug it off, walk away, or basically survive without suffering any internal bleeding, fine. But if the mere thought makes your mouth go dry, your palms cold and clammy and your heart feeling like it's been through Mr. Thurman's meat tenderizer, I say take the gamble and give the relationship your best shot. At worst, you'll end up alone again. At best—" she wiggled her eyebrows "—maybe my mother will be content to teach you how to knit booties and she'll stay off my back for a while longer."

Lisa smiled at Marie's attempt to brighten their mood, and she allowed her to chatter on as she showed her the rest of the changes around the property. But suddenly she was haunted by her friend's suggested question: How *would* she feel if Gabriel walked out of her life tomorrow?

It was almost two hours later when they returned to the house. Lisa went to put on a fresh pot of coffee and Marie wandered from room to room with the freedom of one who feels comfortable in a friend's home. "So, are you packed and ready to leave on the cruise?" Lisa called, getting out the china cups from the cupboard.

"Are you kidding? I've packed and repacked twice already. If Saturday doesn't hurry up and get here, I'm going to end up in the hospital too sick from excitement to go. Hey, this is darling. When did you get it?"

"Get what?" Lisa asked, glancing around the cupboard to where Marie stood by her desk. Her bemused smile turned into a frown when she saw what her friend was holding.

It was a fish on a wooden stand, an exquisitely carved and hand-painted angelfish. Even from where she stood, Lisa was impressed by the detail in the crafts-manship, the realistic fluid lines of the body and the beauty in the coloring. She abandoned the cups and the coffee and went to the living room where she accepted the carving from her friend and stared at it.

"By the look on your face, can I take it you've never seen it before, either?" Marie drawled, pursing her lips in speculation.

"No, I haven't."

"Fascinating." The taller woman adjusted her glasses on her nose and inspected the desk. "No note. I won-der who brought it."

Lisa didn't need a note; she knew who it was from, and even why. It was exactly like the angelfish that had surrounded two honeymooning snorkelers swimming along the coral reefs. They'd spent hours enjoying the tiny creatures' company. And, apparently, after Agent Talbert had delivered Mason Sennett's early birthday present, Gabriel had been reminded that her birthday was fast approaching and he wanted to give her some-thing himself. He'd gone into town a few times to get lumber and supplies, but she didn't know anyplace in town that carried something like this.

"He made it," Marie said.

At Lisa's dazed look, Marie pointed to the carved initials at the back of the base, and Lisa stared at the still-foreign initials. He made it? She didn't even know he had any kind of artistic ability. But what else was new? Wasn't she always saying the man was a walking enigma?

"I think I'd better go."

She glanced up to see Marie heading for the front door. "But I'm making coffee!"

"It's really too hot for coffee. Besides, you have some major thinking to do."

Quickly placing the fish down on her desk, Lisa raced to the door. "Marie, you can't leave," she said, though in all honesty she was more afraid of being alone than in need of company. "I'm not going to see you again until you get back from the cruise. I want to hear more about your plans."

"No, you don't," her friend said with a sage smile. "You've been a good sport to listen to us yacking about it for the past few months as it is. The only reason you're being polite now is that you're scared. Truth is, I'm half tempted to stay. Heaven knows I'm absolutely itching to know what's going on between you two. But I'm a good enough friend to know that now's not the smart time to ask. So, I'm going to take myself down to the town square. I've noticed that new pediatrician, Dr. Garrett, has a tendency to take a late lunch at Neilson's Café. Ruby Ann Potter is his receptionist and she tells me he's newly divorced."

Able at least to summon a chuckle for the dependable way Marie had of keeping the focus of their conversations on men, Lisa hugged her and wished her a good trip. "Tell the others to send me a postcard, too!" she called as Marie climbed into her car.

But as soon as Lisa shut the door, her smile wilted. She returned to the living room where she stood a few cautious feet away from her desk.

It doesn't have supernatural powers, you ninny.

Yet in a way she felt it was calling to her, urging her to reach out and pick it up, stroke its sleek sides, explore the shapely fins that must have been impossibly difficult to carve.

He must have worked on it nights when he'd stubbornly stayed in his cottage, refusing her offer to prepare dinner for them both. She could picture that, his long-fingered hands moving over a virgin block of wood, seeking to mold its natural lines. What had he been thinking? Had it always been his intention to give it to her?

The sound of the coffee beginning to spill over made her run into the kitchen. Grimacing at the mess, she turned off the stove and for the next few minutes concentrated on cleaning up. But still Gabriel's gift pulled her.

She wandered around to the arched entryway separating kitchen from living room and leaned against the wall, warily eyeing the yellow-and-black creature, which seemed to be staring back at her. She remembered the first time they had spotted a small school of angelfish; she had been captivated by them and had almost forgotten to pay attention to how far out she was drifting. Gabriel—she gave herself an inward shake—*Jon*, at first concerned, had later teased her about it and she'd dunked him for laughing at her. Their playfulness had turned into a water fight and then a race for the beach. Near the water's edge he'd scooped her up in his arms and like a marauding buccaneer carried her to their secluded bungalow, where the ensuing lovemaking had been as gritty as the sand still clinging to their bodies. Later, when he saw the effect of that—the raw red scrapes that marred her skin—he'd been surprisingly, adorably apologetic and had swept her into the shower where he'd gently bathed her, soothing her with his hands and his mouth until she'd experienced the sweetest climax possible.

To me he was always giving.

Lisa made an involuntary move as if there was something profound and painful in that realization she wanted to avoid facing. But it was undeniably true; he'd always been a generous husband and lover, not only in a materialistic sense, but in an emotional one.

Guilt, she insisted, trying to interpret his motives. He'd known he was deceiving her, piling up secrets higher than mountains, and the resulting guilt had prompted his generosity.

But he'd more than suffered for it!

Yes, she would have to be blind not to see that he'd paid a price, was paying for it even now. How much longer was she going to hold him at arm's length? How could she expect him to open up to her, share his deepest self with her, when she was keeping her own heart out of reach? Real love wasn't something one could issue in degrees, yet that was what she'd been doing to him ever since his return.

Real loving demanded taking risks. She either had to accept that, go to him wholly and with an open heart, or let him go. The mere prospect left her shaken.

If your mouth goes dry, your palms turn damp and your heart feels like it's been though Mr. Thurman's meat tenderizer...

Lisa hurried toward the back door. Her hand was on the doorknob before she thought to glance down at herself. That brought her to an abrupt halt and she winced.

How could she think of going to him looking like this? She was a mess. First thing that morning she'd caulked the windows in the second cabin and she still had putty under her fingernails; smudges of dirt marked her knees from when she'd been working in the flower beds; and her hair had to be in tangles since she hadn't been near a comb since she got out of bed. Why hadn't Marie said anything? She was usually good for a raised eyebrow or a tactful remark at school if Lisa showed up at lunch with so much as a chalk smudge on her face. Then again, she probably hadn't noticed because she'd been preoccupied with Gabriel. He'd always had a stunning effect on people.

"Blast," she muttered, spinning around and already winding her hair up so that she could tuck it under a towel. "Just what I need—more time to dwell on what a fool I am."

Nine

Despite a keen sense of finality, her knees were shaking. Lisa grew more and more aware of it the closer she came to the cottage. It made her glad she'd decided to put on the pink-and-white wraparound skirt. The hem fell to just below her knees and the cool sleek material was a relief against her tension-riddled body. But by the same token, she wondered if the white halter top was a mistake. Her nervousness and awareness was having another noticeable effect on her body, and the clingy T-shirt material of the halter was only enhancing that. Well, she wouldn't go back and change; as it was, she'd almost talked herself out of doing this twice already.

She passed Pilot, who looked content to spend the rest of the afternoon sleeping beside a hedge of laurel midway between her cottage and Gabriel's. He barely lifted his eyelids as she went by, and Lisa shifted the angelfish between her hands, wishing she had a portion of his calmness.

She also wished she'd left Gabriel's gift back at the house. The way she was gripping it there would be little more than sawdust left by the time she got to his cottage. Her initial reason for taking it along was to provide her with the emotional support she badly needed, but she now realized only Gabriel himself had the power to do that. Still, having this with her did serve to remind her of one good thing—happiness shared.

As nervous as she was, she wasn't about to let herself forget this gift was actually an entreaty to start anew, just as their honeymoon had been a beginning. Back then she hadn't known his work would come between them; now she needed to hear that nothing would take him away again. If she had those words of commitment, she could deal with the rest.

Her slip-on sandals made only the subtlest sound as she climbed the stairs to his front porch, yet Lisa was surprised when that didn't bring him to the screen door. As one of nature's best-trained survivalists, he was too sharp not to sense when someone or something was encroaching on his territory. But even when she peered through the mesh, she saw no sign of him.

"Hello? Anyone home?"

There was no answer, not any sound at all to confirm he was inside. Wondering if he might be off at another part of the property and whether or not she should go look for him, she let herself in. At the same moment the bathroom door opened and Gabriel stepped into the main room of the cottage.

He was in the process of zipping his jeans when he spotted her, and like her, he froze. Water from a shower dripped from his long hair and glistened on his bare chest, his taut abdomen, downward to… She jerked her gaze back to his face. Even though she'd often seen him like this, a powerful sense of awareness and attraction raced through her as though it was for the first time. She was left feeling as flustered and unsure of herself as a virgin walking in on the object of what heretofore had only been a sequestered fantasy.

It didn't help when he glanced down at the angelfish for a long meaningful moment before looking back up to meet her wide-eyed pensive gaze. She saw nothing in that enigmatic eye to give away his inner thoughts, neither a measure of welcome, nor annoyance. As a result, she completely forgot everything she'd been rehearsing to say to him while taking her own shower.

But knowing she had to say something—because it was clear he was going to wait for her to make the first move—she wet her lips and held up the carving like a talisman. "I found your gift…and came to thank you."

For a while it looked as if he was never going to answer, not that she could blame him. Even to her own ears her words had sounded stiff and formal, and about as brilliant as the caught fly in a spider's web announcing it was only passing through.

At last he smoothed back his hair and adjusted his eye patch. "Does that mean you like it?"

"*Very* much. But, um, my birthday isn't for several days yet."

He twisted his lips in a way that only suggested she was on a roll with her quips. "Maybe I should have gotten you something else. Considering the birthdays I've missed, you deserve something far more lavish."

"I love *this*." Her heart fluttered wildly at the look that won her. Her body grew warm, her skin feverishly damp, as if the temperature in the room had just risen ten degrees, though both the ceiling fans in the one-room cottage were rotating. "I—I had no idea you were so talented," she added, wondering how a woman who could remember entire passages of poetry could forget a half-dozen sentences she'd been repeating for the past hour.

"Neither did I, until I realized I needed something to fill my days at the mission." Crossing his arms, he leaned back against the doorjamb, and Lisa wondered if he'd forgotten the top button on his jeans or if he 'd left it unfastened to torment her. "Much to Oscar's disappointment, I showed no calling for missionary work. Trying my hand at carving at least made me feel I was contributing something to the people who'd helped me."

"Knowing you, I'm sure you were already doing more than pulling your own weight around there."

"Knowing me . . ."

There was no missing the touch of sarcasm in his voice. Lisa had the grace to look embarrassed.

"Do you really like it?" he asked.

"It's beautiful. Marie thought so, too."

He glanced around her as if just remembering they'd had a visitor. "Your friend. Has she left?"

Lisa nodded. "We both thought it was of a professional caliber. What I'm trying to say is that there would probably be a demand for your work if you wanted to make some things like this to sell here, as you did in Argentina."

"I hadn't thought of that." He paused, seeming to consider it now. "Bentonville is a small town. Do you really think there would be much of a market?"

"Maybe. Maybe not. At any rate I was thinking more in the line of Gatlinburg. They have a few consignment shops that feature unusual work done by local artists."

"I might look into it. It depends how much time I have."

Disappointment was like a vise squeezing the air from her lungs. What was he saying? Lisa blinked hard, willing the tears that wanted to flood her eyes not to overwhelm her. "Of course. I shouldn't have assumed—"

"I meant that there's still a great deal of renovation work to do. It should take priority for now."

"Oh." The constricting pressure eased and she could breathe again. "Oh," she said again. She knew she sounded dim-witted, but she couldn't help it. In the span of a few seconds he'd snuffed out her hope, only to give it back to her.

"At first I thought about trying my hand at doing a carving of Pilot," he said, breaking into her thoughts. "But I wanted my first gift to you to be representative of something we'd shared."

"Yes," Lisa whispered, gazing down at the angelfish. "I realized that as soon as I saw this." He sounded so in need of reassurance she felt a corresponding pain in her own heart. At least in this they really weren't so different, she thought, taking strength in that new scrap of knowledge. He was groping in the dark as blindly as she was. Reassured, she put his gift on an end table. "I'll always cherish it," she murmured, moving toward him. "But it also makes me feel ashamed. Of my selfishness," she explained, seeing his frown. "Your gift forced me to see how much you've been giving, how much you've been trying to rebuild things between us, while I've done nothing but put up roadblocks. Gabriel, about what happened earlier... I didn't mean to appear embarrassed or ashamed to be with you."

"I know. I let my impatience and frustration make me see things that weren't there. You needn't try to take on guilt for what was my error. You've needed time to deal with the shock that I'd returned. Despite my behavior, I do understand, *querida.*"

"But what I've been trying to ignore is that you've been hurting, too."

Gabriel looked away from her; his chest rose and fell with each deep breath. "I won't deny that was like a knife twisting in my gut."

What was it about admissions from strong people that made them especially poignant? she wondered. As Lisa closed the remaining distance between them and laid her hand against his heart to find its strong beat, she suddenly accepted the reality that she could never have walked away from this man and that he had waited for her long enough. "I wish I had the power to remove those bad moments," she told him quietly. Leaning forward, she nuzzled the dark crinkly hair matting his chest, touched her lips to where his heart pounded furiously. "You've been so patient with me."

"Lisa..." He lifted his hands as if to press her closer, dropped them, then ultimately reached up to stroke her hair. "I need more than your understanding."

"I know."

"Do you really?"

"That's why I'm here."

For an instant his body went ramrod stiff, deathly still. In the next moment it vibrated with a subtle but telling trembling. "Then don't stop," he replied, his voice as ragged as the breath he purged from his lungs. "Even if this is only a dream, don't stop."

"It's not a dream. I want to make love with you. To you."

She couldn't say more because he'd sought and found her lips. But it was all right because Lisa decided to tell him everything else she felt and wanted to share with him in a slow thorough kiss. An uninhibited kiss. They'd already experienced passion, but it had been too long since she'd come to him without fear and doubt and worry.

After an undistinguishable space of time that left her with the sensation of the sea roaring in her ears, and made him shift his hold so that he gripped her waist as if he wanted to absorb her, she withdrew. Just enough to temper the pace, nip at his lower lip, explore the firm sleek texture of him before teasing him with the tenderest of grazings with her teeth. That elicited a guttural groan from him and encouraged her once again to journey deeper.

This time she sought richer darker tastes, invited him, then wantonly lured him into mimicking the erotic mating of her tongue. Heat rose in waves, intensified, and seconds became a minute...then more. Her breath grew shallow, his sounded like a freight train. There was a temptation to race, to surrender, to ease the crescendo of need. Lisa aggressively ignored it and reached for heaven.

Her hands moved like independent restless beings skimming his body, which, already hard, changed into sleek marble. His hands seemed frozen and could only hold her, but it was a grip with a clear message: he wasn't going to let anything stop this until it was over. As Lisa let her body relax completely against him, her corresponding message was equally clear: she didn't want it any other way.

"Take me to bed," she whispered against his lips.

As if he'd been waiting for just those words, he lifted her into his arms. The cottage was one large room with a white louvered-door divider to separate the sleeping area from the living room and kitchen. Gabriel carried her to the bed behind the screen and placed her on the twisted sheets, which betrayed the restless nights that had been plaguing him. He lowered himself beside her. "Do you know how many nights I've lain here wanting, aching for you to walk through that door, to come to me?"

Gently pushing him onto his back, she rose over him, kissed his lips, his scarred cheek and his chin. "I'm here now." And she would show him how much she adored him.

How beautiful he was, she thought, trailing her fingers downward to explore the smoothness of his muscles. He was regaining the weight he'd lost and it was only adding to the powerful magnetism he already exuded. She couldn't resist rediscovering all of him, his biceps, the taut plain of his belly, his steel-hard denim-encased thighs. Wanting to see as much as feel, she slipped out of her sandals and rose to her knees to gaze down his body, caress him with a long sweep of her hair and a gentle stroke of her mouth. When she reached for his zipper, his hand was already untying the bow at her waist. In the space it took for their eyes to meet and share intimate understanding, she had the zipper lowered and he was tossing her skirt across the bed.

She knew every inch of his body almost as well as she knew her own, but she touched him now as if experiencing him for the first time. She needed to make him wholly aware of what this moment meant, not only to her, but to both of them.

Gabriel, however, seemed intent on delivering a message of his own. A low sound of approval had risen from deep within him when he'd seen her lacy pink panties; now he caressed her through them, telling her in a hoarse hot whisper that the silk was no softer, no more exquisite than she was. Then he slid his hands up and down her bare back, drew her over him and splayed his fingers until his palms were stroking the outer swells of her breasts.

"Oh, that feels good," Lisa whispered, duplicating those seductive motions with her hips.

She wanted the moment to continue, but Gabriel had obviously decided that they were still wearing too many clothes and he shifted to untie her halter. It was just as well, she decided; as he began to slip it over her head, she used the opportunity to finish undressing him.

Yet no sooner did she return to him than he rolled her beneath him to close his mouth over her breast. Lisa bowed off the bed, a sigh of pleasure rising to her throat. For a moment she allowed herself the pleasure, the selfishness merely to enjoy. But then she was reminded of what was more important to her at the moment. She gently framed his face with her hands and forced him to look at her. "I want to please *you.*"

"Just being here with you pleases me, don't you understand that by now?" he replied, his gaze as tender as it was possessive.

Lisa shook her head and deftly, mischievously, switched their positions once again. "You ask for too little."

Though she caught a brief glimmer of his surprise, it was soon replaced with a look of naked honesty. "Settling for anything is easy to do when you've lost almost everything. Then every kindness, every tenderness, becomes a doubly valued joy.''

As much as she regretted what she'd made herself deny him, Lisa knew there was no more time for sadness. She wanted to share love with him—and laughter. ''Are you saying,'' she murmured, seductively moving against him, ''there's absolutely no hope of ever spoiling you?''

A wicked gleam flickered in his dark eye. ''None whatsoever. But I could be corrupted,'' he murmured huskily.

Her own smile reflected delight. ''Tell me how?''

''I'm especially vulnerable to the magic of this,'' he said, brushing his thumb across her lower lip. ''And that,'' he added, his voice lowering a whole octave when she drew his finger into her mouth and playfully teased him with her tongue. ''And these,'' he whispered thickly as he caught and kissed each and every one of her gifted fingers.

With her gaze she drank in every nuance of his expression and felt every inch of his arousal and need with her body until her own throbbed not only with a desire to please him, but with a soul-deep commitment to vanquish every bad memory he'd experienced. When she saw his own gaze darken, she knew he was sensing the change in her.

''What is it, *querida?*''

''You. I was just thinking of what a miracle you are to me.''

When he tried to speak, protest, she covered his lips with her own and initiated a kiss that soon had him crushing her to him with a desperation that put an end to the playfulness between them.

"Take me inside you," he demanded, his voice a harsh whisper that only reinforced his need. "Show me."

"Soon." First she had other pleasures to share, blessings to bestow, dreams to realize.

She eased down his body and rose from the bed. Conscious of his gaze devouring her, she brushed that last bit of cloth down over her hips. Then she returned to him, lightly nipping his upraised knee and thigh, caressing him with her hair, exploring with her fingers that part of him where his blood ran the hottest. Love, adoration, longing, all welled in her like an endless spring. Her husband, her lover, her *life*. Feeling the impossible abundance of emotion that brought, she did the only thing she knew to do; she shared it with him, first with her hands and at last with her excruciating gentle mouth.

"Lisa..." She felt his hands in her hair, at first unsteady, then stronger. Her name was a litany of agony and pleasure.

Directed by his urgent touch, she slid up his body and let him guide himself into her. He was so hard, she was so ready, they both gasped at the speed and smoothness of their joining.

Nothing, she thought, would ever feel more perfect than this. Yet she was startled when he sat up, proving how that adjustment only intensified their union. Then he even increased it by coaxing her to wrap her legs around his waist. Feeling him pulsating within her, she wrapped her arms around him and held him close to her heart.

"Now love me," he whispered, again seeking her lips. "Make me forget the hell of missing you. Make me...show me...ah, Lisa...*Lisa*..."

His raw-voiced entreaty ended as she initiated the seductive rhythm that immediately had them clinging to each other with more intensity. She wanted to tell him she knew everything he was feeling. She wanted to tell him she worshipped him, needed him, had been wrong to think she could ever end or forget what was between them. But she was already caught in the storm of sensations and emotions he'd spawned in her. There was only the man and the moment. Closing her eyes, she reached for both.

Home. He'd come home. It was the one profound thought in his mind, even before the fog cleared. For the first time since arriving here, he finally felt as though he had his wife, his home, his *life* back.

Nothing was going to take it from him again.

He exhaled and planted a kiss in the curve of Lisa's shoulder, enjoying the damp salty-sweet taste he found there. "Heaven," he whispered.

"Mmm. Don't speak. I don't want to end this moment. It feels too wonderful."

"*You* feel wonderful," he corrected, stroking her back. She was so fragile in his arms and still too slender, yet no one had ever had such a power to drag the intense emotions from him as she just had. What was also wonderous was that she had come to him, instigated their lovemaking. His spirits spiraled to near euphoria at the thought of that and made him feel half-drunk. "If I'd known all it would take was a prettily painted chunk of wood, I'd have started chopping down trees weeks ago."

"Don't even think that." Lisa chuckled before kissing his chest and raising herself on her arms to search his face. "Seriously, though, I do feel I still owe you an apology."

"Don't be absurd," he murmured, stroking her hair. "For what?"

"For not being honest with myself. For holding you at arm's length. For being an emotional coward. Pick something."

"My love, you had every right to be afraid. How often must I tell you that before you believe me?"

"Well, the truth is, even if you hadn't made me the angelfish, I probably wouldn't have lasted much longer."

"You held out long enough," he growled, then smiled at her moan of despair.

"When I'm making deep dark confessions, you needn't rub it in."

"You're right," he agreed, immediately contrite. "It's just that I'm not sure I still believe this is real, your coming to me as sweetly, as honestly, as you did. And here I was, beginning to think I'd lost you forever." He sighed deeply. "I have a deep dark confession of my own to make. Just before you came I was considering leaving, Lisa."

"No!"

Before, her shock and fear might have given him some sense of satisfaction, but now they only brought him anguish. Never again did he want her to know the pain she'd suffered the last time he'd been forced to leave her. He crushed her to him, feeling her misery as if it was an extension of his own. "I'm not trying to torment you. I only wanted you to know it hurt too much to want what I was beginning to believe I'd never have again."

"That's behind us now. Let's talk about happier things. You're not leaving me. Say it."

"No, sweet." He planted cherishing kisses on her forehead, nose and lips. "Never again."

She rubbed her cheek against his scarred flesh. "When I think what you went through, I can't bear it. If I'd have been able to, I would have willingly taken your pain."

He could hear the depth of her emotion in the huskiness of her voice, and he rolled her beneath him, stroked her hair. "Hush, my angel, it's over. Let's put the past behind us. Why dwell on it when there's a future to plan—and love to share," he added, once more tempted to taste her lips.

This kiss held promise and commitment and soon had Lisa moaning softly and pressing closer to him. "Don't start something you won't have time to finish."

"Who says I won't?" he asked with a touch of his old confidence.

"Me." Looking well-loved, she stretched beneath him. "I thought we could go to the house. I want to cook us dinner."

"You can think of food at a time like this?"

"I'm starving, aren't you?"

He looked deeply into her eyes. "Ravenous—though food isn't necessarily at the top of my list of cravings."

Laughing, Lisa surprised him by agilely maneuvering from beneath him. Sitting up, she reached for her clothes. She was exquisite, he thought, his heart wrenching as he imagined how differently things could have turned out. Fate wasn't always generous enough to allow people a second chance. *I'll never risk losing you or your love again,* he vowed silently, reaching out to caress one of her up-tilted breasts before her clothing hid her from his sight.

"Maybe we should discuss what we're going to have," he murmured, deciding she was in too big a rush to leave him. He tried to draw her back down beside him, but she was determined.

"I want to prepare you the dinner we should have had that first night," she insisted. "Why don't you take a nap and come to the house in about an hour? I know you could use the rest after the day you put in," she added, leaning close to placate him with a kiss.

"All right." Resigned to letting her have her way, at least in this, he leaned back against the pillows and appeased himself by watching her finish dressing. "But only an hour, no more."

However, only minutes after she left, Gabriel realized there was no way he was going to sleep. Not because he wasn't pleasantly tired. Lisa was right; work, fresh air and their lovemaking had left him feeling wonderfully lethargic. But something else held sleep at bay. Some dark cloud, some sixth sense or indescribable something, was triggering an uneasiness in him. He tried to shrug it off as conditioned self-doubt; having never expected to know this kind of happiness again, it only seemed logical that he should expect something to go wrong. On the other hand what was there to go wrong?

Yet he sensed trouble. Something was not quite as it should be.

He swung his feet over the side of the bed and grabbed for his jeans. It wouldn't hurt to take a look around, if only to placate himself.

Outside, a late-afternoon lull had settled over the area. There was no sign of Pilot, but that only meant the pooch had probably decided to follow his mistress into the house in the hopes of mooching a snack.

Gabriel glanced to the right and considered taking a walk out back. It would kill time and it wouldn't hurt to check the cottages. Maybe Lisa had left on a light or opened a window when she'd been showing her friend around; there was no need to tempt a squirrel or raccoon to climb inside and make a mess. Or maybe he'd left an electric tool plugged in at the second cottage. He'd been so keyed up about Lisa's withdrawal back then, he hadn't been concentrating on work as he should have—

Lisa's scream followed by a crash cut off his wandering thoughts. Terror gripped his heart. Even as Pilot started barking, Gabriel was lunging off the porch.

He instinctively circled the cottage and stayed hidden in the trees, the way he had when Talbert had come to call. Only now his heart was pounding as if he'd just run a marathon. Dear God, what had happened? What was wrong?

Because of the warm weather, Lisa kept most of the windows in the house open, so he made his way to her bedroom, knowing that was his best chance to get in without being observed. As he carefully removed the screen, he wished he'd had time to retrieve the gun hidden in his cabin. Well, he would just have to work around that.

He'd never been thrilled that her windows were so close to the ground, but as he eased inside, he decided to overlook that fact this once. From down the hallway came the sound of voices, indiscernible due to Pilot's bellowing. After a moment, he could make out what Lisa was saying. She was trying to calm Pilot and apologizing. Apologizing?

Barefooted, Gabriel tiptoed to the doorway. He was acutely aware of the beads of sweat already dotting his brow. All he needed was one board to creak beneath his weight and someone, at least Pilot, would pick up on it. At the door he carefully peered around the corner... and saw him.

The man stood with his back to him. Because of the hour, the house was cast in shadows, so it was impossible to see details. He appeared to have come though the front door and had obviously startled Lisa, causing her to drop the vase she'd been carrying. Apparently on her way back to the house, she'd stopped to pick some flowers and had only just got them into water. The living room floor was a mess, with water, flowers and glass everywhere. She was crouching, collecting the biggest pieces while trying to control Pilot who looked intent on sinking his teeth into their intruder's substantial muscles.

There was something about the man, who now shifted and was half-hidden by the wall, that disturbed Gabriel. It wasn't only his size, which was considerable; despite the expensive business suit he wore, he exuded a square-shouldered military aura.

Gabriel didn't waste time looking around the bedroom for a weapon, though with his training just about anything would do. His hands would be adequate, he decided, if he could get close enough before he was spotted.

"It's nothing really valuable," Lisa was assuring him. "You just startled me, that's all. *Pilot*, will you please *shut up*."

Gabriel decided he was going to have to have a chat with her about being overly friendly with intruders. Stay still, he willed the stranger. Just a few more feet...

The intruder muttered something and gestured, reaching up to scratch the back of his neck. "I should have—"

Gabriel saw him tense, knew he'd sensed that someone was behind him. In the instant Gabriel made his move, so did the other man and Gabriel realized he knew him—but it was too late to withdraw without suffering an injury.

With a sureness that had come from years of practice, he grabbed the man's right wrist with his left hand and twisted it counterclockwise. Simultaneously, he used his right hand to push the man's upper arm to the left. The intruder grunted with pain, and Gabriel used his involuntary jerk toward the left to force his face against the wall. Fully anticipating a retaliatory move, Gabriel shifted to avoid the intruder's effort to crush a heel into his instep.

"Easy, or I'll put you on your knees," Gabriel ordered, using his right hand to reach for the gun he was confident he would find at the small of the man's back. Only then did he completely release him and step back into the room. "Are you all right?" he asked Lisa, though he didn't dare take his eyes off their visitor's back.

"Of course she is," the man answered, rubbing his sore arm. He sounded more disgusted with himself than offended by Gabriel's insinuation. "I only surprised her when I walked in the front door without knocking."

"You're supposed to keep it locked, *querida*," Gabriel told his wife with a gentle rebuke.

"But I thought it was."

"Yes—" Gabriel smiled crookedly "—no doubt you're right. I'm sure the doorbell is in working order, as well. Why don't you let Pilot out back before we all go deaf."

As she followed his suggestion, their visitor shifted slightly to speak over his shoulder. "Mind if I turn around now? I thought there was only one SOB who was good enough to pull a move like that on me. I'd like to face the man who just proved me wrong."

"Why not," Gabriel replied. "But, remember, no sudden moves. I'd hate to have to send you home in a sling or on crutches."

In reply the man raised his hands in surrender, then slowly turned around. Like his shoulders, his face was square, roughly handsome and hard as granite. It was framed by conservatively cut thick hair that Gabriel knew would be the color of sable in the sun. His eyes were the cold gray of gunmetal, but noticeable for only a second before he narrowed them as he found himself looking down the bore of his own .9mm Beretta.

Gabriel smiled with equal coldness. "*¿Qué pasa, compadre?* Not a pretty sight, eh?"

Ten

"**S**weet Georgia Brown," Mason Sennett rasped, slowly lowering his hands to his sides. "Jon?"

Gabriel eased the hammer forward on the automatic and handed it back to his old friend. "You could at least have pretended to take a while, *amigo*. You're going to make Lisa feel bad that it took her almost twenty-four hours."

Sennett glanced apologetically at Lisa who, Gabriel noticed with no small concern, was watching them like someone trapped in a nightmare. "Don't feel bad, honey. I knew him a helluva long time before you ever met him. I'll admit that voice threw me, but like I said, there's only been one man who could ever sneak up on me. And once I turned around..." He returned to studying Gabriel and, finally the dismay he felt for his friend showed in the deepening lines around his eyes and mouth.

"Don't worry about it," Gabriel said, when it was clear Mason didn't know how to continue. "I can soak my head in battery acid and I'd still be prettier than you."

It had been an ongoing joke between them. Sennett was a big muscular man whose very presence made it impossible to ignore him, and he'd never had problems attracting more than his share of female attention. But whenever Gabriel had been anywhere in the vicinity, except for an occasional remark about the shrewdness of his gray eyes or the girth of his massive chest, Mason might as well have been part of the furniture.

"In fact you're starting to look as domesticated as that old hound your wife bought when you insisted she get a guard dog," Gabriel added, accepting that it was going to take his friend a moment to get over his shock.

Mason's eyes took on a suspicious brightness, but he tried to oblige his friend by trading insults. "You look like you took a first class tour through hell."

"It's the first time I wouldn't have complained about getting a cheap seat. It's good to see you, *compadre.*"

"Good? Hell," Mason said, closing the distance between them and hauling him close for a bear hug. "It's damned fantastic!"

The men embraced with an intensity that celebrated not only friendship but survival. When Mason once again put Gabriel at arm's distance, the brightness in his eyes expanded to wet his eyelashes. "I burned bridges trying to find you, man."

"I know." Gabriel would have done the same if their situations had been reversed.

Mason lifted one huge hand and, with surprising gentleness, touched the corner of Gabriel's eye patch. "Was it a bomb?"

"You'd think someone would teach idiots using explosives to do a decent job."

"Hey, I don't want to hear any more of that kind of crap." Like an elder brother, Mason hugged him again, cupping the back of Gabriel's head with a poignant tenderness that had Gabriel clenching his teeth against the knot forming in his own throat. "Hell, we're going to be crying like two old women in a minute," Mason growled as they awkwardly parted. "And look at that mop of hair. You're turning into a hippie—a gray-haired hippie!"

"At least it's natural," Gabriel drawled, knowing full well that Mason's hair was, too. Just as quickly the teasing mood between them died. "You never quite bought the medical examiner's report, did you?"

The big man hung his head. "Logic told me I should, but somehow I just couldn't swallow it."

"Is that the main reason you kept tabs on Lisa?"

"You know damned well I would have kept tabs on her no matter what," Mason replied testily.

"It just made it more worth your while, because you thought if I was going to show up one day, it would probably be near her. Come to think of it, I owe you a few loose teeth for opening your big mouth to her in the first place."

Mason shifted his gaze to Lisa. "Honey, hold your hands over your ears a minute. It seems that explosion must have knocked some of the boy's brains out and I need to explain some home truths to him." He shoved his gun back into his belt holster and poked a finger at Gabriel's chest. "I'll admit I knew that if anyone could have survived the mess you were in, you could. But I would have kept tabs on her regardless, because we were pals. Got it? And furthermore, she had a right to know the truth about you. I told you that when you announced you were going to marry her. Hell, if anyone has a right to be angry it's me. I got cheated out of kissing the bride."

Gabriel considered that for a moment and finally, somberly, inclined his head. Then he glanced at the scowling man from beneath one stark eyebrow. "You even think about making up for lost opportunities, I'll punch your lights out."

"She had a rough time of it," Mason told him when the laughter once again died between them. "So why the phantom act all this time?"

"He...he was hurt, Mason," Lisa said before Gabriel could reply. "It was a long time before he was in any condition to come back."

"I want to hear all about it," Mason replied, as Gabriel held his wife's gaze. "A complete briefing."

"An unofficial one," Gabriel corrected, turning back to him. "Remember Jonathan Howard has been classified as deceased."

"You know it was Talbert who pricked my interest and made me come down here. There was something about a not-too-friendly guy named Ballesteros hanging around here that pushed me to see for myself. Well, we'll discuss identities later. First I want to hear what information you can give me about the situation down there."

"Not much you'd be interested in."

"I'll take what I can get. Your speculations were often more useful than other agents' full investigations."

"How's Sabra?" Gabriel asked, knowing this kind of talk could only be upsetting Lisa.

He watched his friend's eyes change at the mention of his wife, saw the rush of stark love and tenderness and wondered if he looked the same when speaking about Lisa. Love—what it could do to a man.

"Gorgeous as ever but about as flexible as a bullet out of that Beretta. I'm trying to convince her that we should work on another kid, and she's threatened to lock me out of our bedroom if I so much as mention it again."

"That'll be the day. She loves kids."

"Yeah, but I've been traveling a lot more lately and she's made it clear she doesn't intend to raise them on her own. Well, pour us a drink and let's negotiate. I want to talk to you about a situation in Brazil that's giving me hell. There's a—"

At the sound of the back door opening and closing, Gabriel spun around to see Lisa walking away from the house. He swore softly. "Lisa!"

He started to go after her, but Mason grabbed his arm. "Let her have a few minutes alone."

"No way, pal. I nearly lost her a second time because of the secrets I kept from her."

"I can imagine. But right now it's better if she isn't around. Some of what I have to say is for your ears only—and you have some big choices to make."

Lisa could hardly see through the blur of tears, and she ignored Pilot who followed on her heels like a morose puppy. She could barely see in front of her, but she managed to climb the stairs to Gabriel's cottage without breaking her neck.

Dying. She felt as though she was dying. Again.

She couldn't go through this again. Surely he wouldn't ask her to.

She'd been afraid for him when she realized he'd crept into the house. Mason was such a big man; what if he'd reacted differently? What if Gabriel had been hurt? And then those few seconds when she watched her husband holding a gun on his best friend had been like something out of a spy novel. Only this had been real.

Once they'd embraced she began to relax—until she started to sense that perhaps friendship was more durable than marriage vows. Between that and Gabriel's obvious attraction to life on the edge, how could she hope to compete?

She couldn't, she realized, gazing at the bed where only a short while ago they'd made love. She saw that as clearly as she knew she'd never had a choice in loving him.

Spinning away, her gaze fell on the worktable across the room. She hadn't noticed it before. Where had it come from and when had he set it in here? she wondered, wandering toward it.

On top was another carving. He'd only just started it, but already Lisa could tell it was a woman, nude except for the long hair that flowed to her waist. Though barely more than a rough form at this point, she could already tell who it was supposed to represent, and her tears began to flow heavier.

"Oh, Gabriel..."

How was she going to let him go? Already she felt as though her heart was being torn in two.

Yet would their love survive if she begged him to stay as she almost had already? This was her choice of homes, but not necessarily his. He might feel isolated, trapped here. He loved her, she had no doubt, but he was also a brilliant man with deep principles and a strong sense of obligation. Maybe his work wasn't anything she would ever fully understand, and maybe it was at times ugly as he'd said, but she would never believe that he didn't approach his part in it with honor. If he felt committed to returning to that life, what right did she have to hold him back?

There was only one thing to do, she told herself, brutally wiping the tears from her face with the backs of her hands. She went to the closet and found his canvas satchel. Setting it on the bed, she began to pack his things.

When Gabriel walked in a few minutes later, she was just zipping it closed. He looked from it to her tear-stained face and took a deep breath.

"It's all right," she told him, her voice husky with suppressed emotion. "I won't make it difficult for you."

"You won't?" he asked cautiously, now glancing from the bag to the open bureau to the bathroom. "I'm not sure I understand."

Her laugh was forced. "It looks pretty obvious to me."

"Lisa, let's sit down. You're on the edge of hysteria."

"I don't want to sit down. I've made up my mind. If this is what you want, then who am I to stand in your way?"

"You want me to leave?"

She clenched her hands into fists. "I want you to do what you feel you must."

"I thought I was," he replied quietly.

Lisa had to close her eyes at that. Sweet liar. She would treasure that once he was gone, but right now it was making her lifeblood pour from the wound in her heart. "Gabriel, let's not prolong this, all right? I'm not very good at it yet. But I promise I'll try to get better. Go. And if, when your work is finished, whenever it's finished, I'll be here waiting."

He stood there for several endless seconds, until she thought she was going to scream, until she thought she was going to break down and tell him she'd changed her mind and couldn't go through with it. But finally he picked up the bag and murmuring, "All right," he walked out.

Lisa spun around and stared after him in disbelief. That was it? "All right" and he was leaving? Her pain turned to fury.

She went after him. "Gabriel!"

Ignoring her, he headed straight for the house. Lisa dreaded the idea of Mason's witnessing this, but then again if he didn't want to listen, he could always go wait in his car.

However, once she got inside, she realized Mason was already gone. What was more shocking was that Gabriel was carrying his bag down the hall. He disappeared into her room.

Upset, distraught, confused, Lisa followed and entered the bedroom just as he set the bag on the chest at the base of the bed.

"What are you doing?" she demanded.

Gabriel turned calmly and crossed to her. "I think that's fairly obvious."

"Well, it isn't," she said, brushing away his hands as he reached for her. But he was persistent. "Gabriel, stop it!"

"You stop it," he replied, this time trapping her against him and lowering them both onto the bed. "Stop trying to be noble and stop ignoring what's before your eyes. I'm moving in. And in about one minute I'm going to make love to you."

"But Mason—"

"—is gone, though he'll be back later. I told him we needed an hour alone to clear up some misunderstandings."

"And then you'll be leaving with him?"

"No, my adorable dimwit, I will not. I told you I'm staying and I meant it."

"But he wants you back."

"He also has aspirations of becoming secretary of defense. At least he might get that wish." He smiled crookedly. "Didn't you believe what I told you before?"

"Yes . . . no . . . oh, I wanted to." She framed his face with her hands. "Are you serious? You really want to stay? You're not just saying this because you think it's what I want to hear?"

"This is where my heart is. This is where you are. How can I leave?" He took her left hand and touched his lips to the ring she'd never taken off. "Thank you for this. Whenever I lost hope over the past few weeks, I only had to see this to find the courage to continue. Now don't you think it's time you gave me the words I've been longing to hear since the day you opened your door to me?"

Fresh tears slipped down the sides of her face into her hair. "I love you. I never stopped. I never will. *I love you,*" she whispered holding him fiercely.

"And I love you, *querida,*" he replied, burying his face in her hair. "Ah, it feels wonderful to finally be able to say it. I'd believed I'd lost the right forever."

He kissed her then, deeply, hungrily. As always it spawned the flames of longing that soon had them pressing closer with growing need.

"Do you think I would have been able to resist you indefinitely?" Lisa asked, stroking the long muscles of his back.

"I thought, I hoped I could make you want me, but I wasn't sure it was enough to convince you to give me everything I needed."

"Which is?"

"A wife. Will you marry me, my love?"

"I already am your wife," she reminded him. "Remember you said as much yourself."

"True. But I want it to look right in the eyes of the world, as well. And for our children," he added, already visualizing how radiant she would look when she carried their child. The idea was both spiritually uplifting and sensually inspiring. And then Lisa was kissing him, forcing his thoughts to more immediate joys.

"Is it true? Are we going to be allowed to live in peace?"

"Mason will growl and threaten, but it's true."

"And you'll be content to live here?"

"I told you before, I would have settled anywhere you'd gone. However, yes, I think you chose well. We'll manage nicely. And if my carvings are received with half as much enthusiasm as you seem to think . . ."

"They will, you'll see."

"I've started one I doubt I'll ever want to share, though."

"I saw it," she told him, her eyes beginning to twinkle. "And I'm impressed with your memory."

"Well, I'll admit it would inspire me to have the real woman as a model."

"Oh, I'd love to pose for you."

Her faith and enthusiasm made his heart swell and his eye burn with tears. To hide it, he kissed her. "My life, my love..."

"I want you."

He wanted her, too, was in fact already reaching for the bow at her waist, eager to rediscover the sleek curves and generous warmth that was an integral part of her. As he removed her clothes, she removed his. This time there was no necessity for foreplay. They merged as if they'd been wanting this from the moment they'd left his cottage, as indeed they had.

It wasn't going to last long, they knew that, too, so when Gabriel raised himself on his forearms, linked his hands with hers and gazed into her face, his possessive smile held a touch of sheepishness.

"I adore you," he murmured.

"And I you."

Afterward, he whispered aloud the words that said everything for him. "I'm home, little dove. I'm finally home."

"Yes, my brave soldier." Lisa kissed him and held him close.

*   *   *   *   *

Bestselling author **NORA ROBERTS** captures all the romance, adventure, passion and excitement of Silhouette in a special miniseries.

THE
CALHOUN WOMEN

Four charming, beautiful and fiercely independent sisters set out on a search for a missing family heirloom—an emerald necklace—and each finds something even more precious . . . passionate romance.

Look for THE CALHOUN WOMEN miniseries starting in June.

COURTING CATHERINE
in Silhouette Romance #801 (June/$2.50)

A MAN FOR AMANDA
in Silhouette Desire #649 (July/$2.75)

FOR THE LOVE OF LILAH
in Silhouette Special Edition #685 (August/$3.25)

SUZANNA'S SURRENDER
in Silhouette Intimate Moments #397 (September/$3.25)

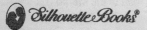 *Silhouette Books*®

MILLION DOLLAR JACKPOT
SWEEPSTAKES RULES & REGULATIONS
NO PURCHASE NECESSARY TO ENTER OR RECEIVE A PRIZE

1 Alternate means of entry: Print your name and address on a 3"×5" piece of plain paper and send to the appropriate address below.

In the U.S.	In Canada
MILLION DOLLAR JACKPOT	MILLION DOLLAR JACKPOT
P.O. Box 1867	P.O. Box 609
3010 Walden Avenue	Fort Erie, Ontario
Buffalo, NY 14269-1867	L2A 5X3

2. To enter the Sweepstakes and join the Reader Service, affix the Four Free Books and Free Gifts sticker along with both of your other Sweepstakes stickers to the Sweepstakes Entry Form. If you do not wish to take advantage of our Reader Service, but wish to enter the Sweepstakes only, do not affix the Four Free Books and Free Gifts sticker; affix only the Sweepstakes stickers to the Sweepstakes Entry Form. Incomplete and/or inaccurate entries are ineligible for that section or sections of prizes. Torstar Corp. and its affiliates are not responsible for mutilated or unreadable entries or inadvertent printing errors. Mechanically reproduced entries are null and void.

3. Whether you take advantage of this offer or not, on or about April 30, 1992, at the offices of D.L. Blair, Inc., Blair, NE, your sweepstakes numbers will be compared against the list of winning numbers generated at random by the computer. However, prizes will only be awarded to individuals who have entered the Sweepstakes. In the event that all prizes are not claimed, a random drawing will be held from all qualified entries received from March 30, 1990 to March 31, 1992, to award all unclaimed prizes. All cash prizes (Grand to Sixth) will be mailed to winners and are payable by check in U.S. funds. Grand prize will be shipped to winners via third-class mail. These prizes are in addition to any free, surprise or mystery gifts that might be offered. Versions of this Sweepstakes with different prizes of approximate equal value may appear at retail outlets or in other mailings by Torstar Corp. and its affiliates.

4. PRIZES: (1) *Grand Prize $1,000,000.00 Annuity; (1) First Prize $25,000.00; (1) Second Prize $10,000.00; (5) Third Prize $5,000.00; (10) Fourth Prize $1,000.00; (100) Fifth Prize $250.00; (2,500) Sixth Prize $10.00; (6,000) **Seventh Prize $12.95 ARV.

   *This presentation offers a Grand Prize of a $1,000,000.00 annuity. Winner will receive $33,333.33 a year for 30 years without interest totalling $1,000,000.00.

   **Seventh Prize: A fully illustrated hardcover book, published by Torstar Corp. Approximate Retail Value of the book is $12.95.

   Entrants may cancel the Reader Service at any time without cost or obligation (see details in Center Insert Card).

5. Extra Bonus! This presentation offers an Extra Bonus Prize valued at $33,000.00 to be awarded in a random drawing from all qualified entries received by March 31, 1992. No purchase necessary to enter or receive a prize. To qualify, see instructions in Center Insert Card. Winner will have the choice of any of the merchandise offered or a $33,000.00 check payable in U.S. funds. All other published rules and regulations apply.

6. This Sweepstakes is being conducted under the supervision of D.L. Blair, Inc. By entering the Sweepstakes, each entrant accepts and agrees to be bound by these rules and the decisions of the judges, which shall be final and binding. Odds of winning the random drawing are dependent upon the number of entries received. Taxes, if any, are the sole responsibility of the winners. Prizes are nontransferable. All entries must be received at the address on the detachable Business Reply Card and must be postmarked no later than 12:00 MIDNIGHT on March 31, 1992. The drawing for all unclaimed Sweepstakes prizes and for the Extra Bonus Prize will take place on May 30, 1992, at 12:00 NOON at the offices of D.L. Blair, Inc., Blair, NE.

7. This offer is open to residents of the U.S., United Kingdom, France and Canada, 18 years or older, except employees and immediate family members of Torstar Corp., its affiliates, subsidiaries and all other agencies, entities and persons connected with the use, marketing or conduct of this Sweepstakes. All Federal, State, Provincial, Municipal and local laws apply. Void wherever prohibited or restricted by law. Any litigation within the Province of Quebec respecting the conduct and awarding of a prize in this publicity contest must be submitted to the Régie des Loteries et Courses du Québec.

8. Winners will be notified by mail and may be required to execute an affidavit of eligibility and release, which must be returned within 14 days after notification or an alternate winner may be selected. Canadian winners will be required to correctly answer an arithmetical, skill-testing question administered by mail, which must be returned within a limited time. Winners consent to the use of their name, photograph and/or likeness for advertising and publicity in conjunction with this and similar promotions without additional compensation.

9. For a list of our major prize winners, send a stamped, self-addressed envelope to: MILLION DOLLAR WINNERS LIST, P.O. Box 4510, Blair, NE 68009. Winners Lists will be supplied after the May 30, 1992 drawing date.

Offer limited to one per household.

LTY-S791

SILHOUETTE·INTIMATE·MOMENTS®

IT'S TIME TO MEET
THE MARSHALLS!

In 1986, bestselling author Kristin James wrote A VERY SPECIAL FAVOR for the Silhouette Intimate Moments line. Hero Adam Marshall quickly became a reader favorite, and ever since then, readers have been asking for the stories of his two brothers, Tag and James. At last your prayers have been answered!

In August, look for THE LETTER OF THE LAW (IM #393), James Marshall's story. If you missed youngest brother Tag's story, SALT OF THE EARTH (IM #385), you can order it by following the directions below. And, as our very special favor to you, we'll be reprinting A VERY SPECIAL FAVOR this September. Look for it in special displays wherever you buy books.

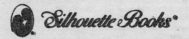